THE CRYING DANCE

No matter what God you believe in, there is always a larger God. No matter what name you call God, the name is always incorrect.

Wu Jiyan
Elements of Being

THE CRYING DANCE

John Spivey

CROWSCRY PRESS
Santa Barbara, California

The Crying Dance

By John Spivey

Published by:

CrowsCry Press

4732 Ashdale St.

Santa Barbara, California 93110

The poem "Still in the Mountains"
Used by permission of
John Dofflemyer

ISBN-13: 978-0-9765691-4-5

Library of Congress Control Number: 2014935818

Book and Cover Production by Dowitcher Designs,
Santa Barbara, California

Front cover and dedication page credits:
Stronghold—Due East from Moro Rock

Lithograph © 2008 by Matthew Rangel

*For the Kaweah River
its tributaries, distributaries,
and mountains that feed it
and
for Barbara and Danica*

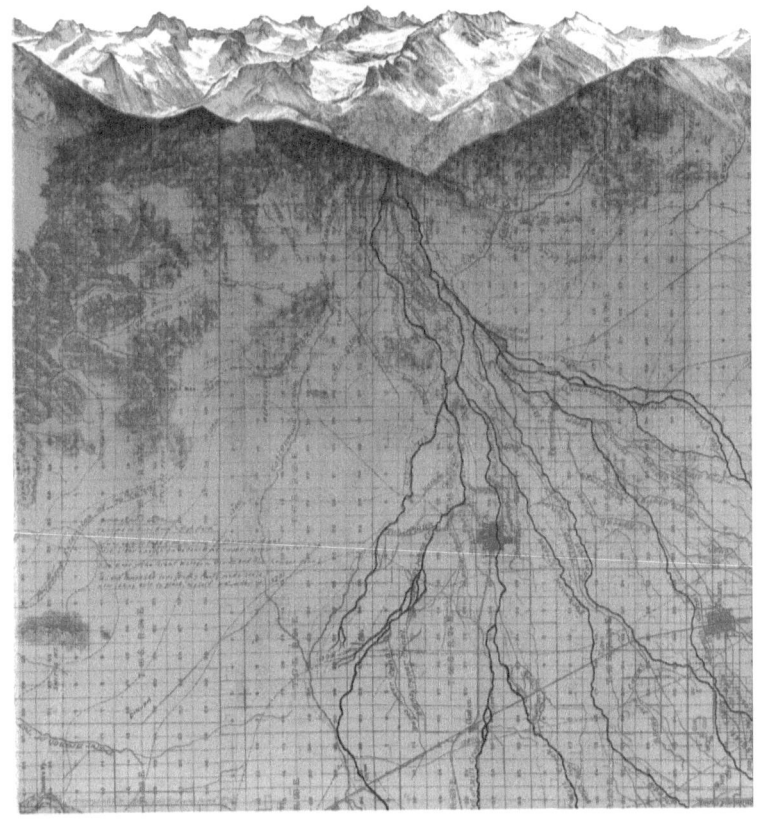

CONTENTS

FOREWORD

"The past is never dead. It isn't even past"

William Faulkner

Upon first reading an early draft of the book you hold in your hands I was so moved that I wept, turning my face into the pitch black airplane window to maintain my privacy. I felt in that moment like an orphan learning where he came from and who his people were. For beyond all else, with *The Crying Dance*, John Spivey tells for the first time the true story of the place where I grew up.

It is a place that is easy to hate. Flat and generally dull of aspect, scorching in summer, foggy in winter, polluted in all seasons, ridden with crime and poverty, it's a place where few people live by choice. And yet, since earliest childhood, I have always loved the fields and dusty hills where the San Joaquin Valley meets the first uncertain crest of the Sierra Nevada. *The Crying Dance* goes a long way toward explaining my emotions. I wish every high school kid in the valley who dreams of getting out, or who knows they will never be able to leave, could be given Spivey's book as required reading, so that—leaving or staying—they would better understand the full brunt of historical trauma that has separated them from their true inheritance of well-being. And if someday the last of the vineyards and orchards have been torn up and replaced by cookie-cutter tract homes and strip malls, if the crime and the smog worsen, I hope at least one edition of *The Crying Dance* finds its way into the hands of someone who can be inspired to tell others: *it was not always this way, it did not have to end like this, this was once one of the most balanced and beautiful places on Earth.*

When I was a young man intent on being a novelist myself, I thought I would write a book about where I grew up, the flat valley lands between the Kings and Kaweah Rivers south of Fresno. In a place where all the vineyards, orchards and roads run due north-south or east-west, and where as a child I was fascinated by anything in the landscape that wasn't straight—say a road with an unexpected turn—I roughed out the draft of a book I thought to entitle *The Place Where Nothing Ever Happened.* Like everyone around me—young and old alike—I assumed the world we lived in had always been the way it appeared now. We had no past worth recounting. Settlers had come to an empty valley, tilled the soil and built the little rag tag towns that clung to the old rail lines. That was the whole story as far as we knew. On clear days we could see the huge snow crested Sierra. They were altogether different from the Valley, but they also had no history. In fact, because they were set aside as National Parks and forests they also seemed like a place where nothing had ever happened. They were wild and beautiful and gave birth to roaring rivers. But upon entering the valley these rivers dissolved into a maze of canals and ditches that branched again and again into nothing, as if to say that all remarkable things come to pedestrian ends. Nothing went anywhere.

As a psychiatrist I've learned from both experience and research that nothing in life is straight and that people and places that appear to lack a past are almost always hiding trauma. The truest story of people and places, and the first step in their redemption, comes from remembering this forgotten past—both the good that was lost and the bad that occurred.

I say *The Crying Dance* is the first true history of my homeland because it is the first great effort at remembering who we were and how we came to be who we are now. That it is full of magical realism only makes its gritty truths and hard won story of redemption the more real and powerful.

Like life itself, *The Crying Dance* is full of surprises and contradictions. It offers itself as a tale of redemption for JR—the iconic loner—a cowboy with a poet's soul. JR carries the wounds of his damaging childhood exacerbated by recent war experiences that leave him unable to do anything but isolate himself in the foothills, a middle zone between the regenerative fecundity of the valley and the spiritual release of the high mountains. Through the story's remarkable series of twists and turns, we realize a deep truth: redemption can never be an individual affair. It always requires reconnection with those around us, both the living as well as the dead. Those who set out to redeem JR learn, in turn, that it is he who must redeem them, and that only by doing so will he himself be redeemed.

Of all places in America, none is more removed from its Native American roots than Central California. Its history is brought to life in all its complexity and tragedy in *The Crying Dance*. Although the area was largely overlooked during the Spanish colonization of the coast, the Native populations of the San Joaquin Valley were ravaged by foreign diseases for 100 years before gold was discovered to the north in 1849. Ultimately the Americans paid bounties for dead Indians, whether they were men, women or children. During the 1840s Francisco, one of *The Crying Dance's* major protagonists, comes to take his place as a chief of the Kaweah tribe. When the Valley came to be settled in earnest in the late

1870s and 80s the Native peoples who had loved and tended the landscape were already gone, with little trace of their existence left behind. Hence, of all places in the country, the Central Valley best matched the vision of American expansion—empty land free for the taking. Today we are the inheritors of this great emptiness, the same emptiness that JR must face and overcome in *The Crying Dance*. That he requires two semi-immortal beings who live in the mountains to do this doesn't seem entirely implausible given the enormity of the task.

I said at the beginning of this foreword that despite its manifold failings, I have always loved the place from which I come. Anyone who knows me will appreciate the depth of this understatement. Although I left the valley for good when I turned 18, I have never been able to really "leave" it, and have come back repeatedly over the years to drive its roads, wander its fields and trace the course of its constrained rivers. I love the valley as if it were a person.

But for all the years of doing this, I never really saw the valley for what it was until I came upon Spivey's books. Now where I once saw only fields and straight-arrow roads, I see the lost remains of Indian villages. When I gaze into the canals and ditches, I see water that once teamed with salmon and enormous sturgeon. In the few oak trees that still dot the landscape I see a hint of what was once a massive oak forest inhabited by bear and wolf and wolverine. Up in the hills, where new little ranchettes threaten to overwhelm the old ways of life, I see a valley where the Native peoples came for one last great gathering in 1870. They came to call their dead back to life in a ceremony known popularly as the Ghost Dance. The Ghost Dance? Who knew such things ever occurred in a place where nothing ever happened? Where the hills meet the valley, the Kaweah River is impounded by Terminus Dam. The lackluster lake it forms fills with houseboats and jet skis in hot weather. Before *The Crying Dance,* I valued the spot largely for its association with a high school girl I loved from afar and once saw there in a bikini. But now I know that the dam hides an ancient cave where the Indians came to seek visions and where the characters in *The Crying Dance* come to understand their interwoven fates.

As much as I have valued *The Crying Dance* for giving me back the history of the place that formed me, and by doing so healing some of my own sense of disconnection and pain, I came to realize its full gift to me earlier this year on the other side of the world. I was in Melbourne, Australia, to deliver a lecture to the Australasian Society for Psychiatric Research Society. The lecture done, I considered my sightseeing options. The afternoon was rainy so I decided to check out the new Aborigine exhibit at the city's museum. The exhibit has received rave reviews and for good reason. It is probably the best presentation of indigenous life that I have ever seen: beautiful, evocative and informative all at once.

Certainly no people on earth were more exotic, more foreign, than the aboriginal peoples of Australia. And yet, as I stood amidst the displays moved by the beauty of their ancient way of life, I had a shock of sudden recognition. I realized I knew these people. I knew how they looked at things. I knew how they felt about the land. I knew how they cared for it by burning and scattering seeds. This is difficult to put into words because it wasn't just a sense of book knowledge. I felt a deep kinship with their perspective of the world. I asked myself, how had this knowing happened? In a flash I realized that I felt a connection with them because I had first come to feel a connection with the lost indigenous world of Central California. And this connection, in turn, had occurred because of how John Spivey had helped me recover something I had never even realized was lost: my ancestors. Not my flesh and blood ancestors, but the ancestral ways of how we had once lived in the world.

At the end of the day, *The Crying Dance* is about how so many things that seem disconnected and barren are in fact deeply connected and full of beautiful, sometimes heart-breaking life. And, the deepest connections harken back to those old ancestral ways that sustained human existence over tens of thousands of years, and that I increasingly believe we must recover if we are to live whole lives in the modern world. The Crying Dance doesn't leave it at that, however, for just as we need the ancient ones, they also need us to heal their wounds. Thus, just as JR can't understand himself until he comes to understand how his forbears pillaged and destroyed the Native world, Francisco, who embodies that ancient world, can't understand himself fully until he comes to understand JR.

Finally, did I mention that *The Crying Dance* is a hell of a good love story?

Charles L. Raison, MD
Professor
Department of Psychiatry
College of Medicine
Barry and Janet Lang Professor
John and Doris Norton School of Family and Consumer Sciences
University of Arizona
Tucson, AZ

THE INVOCATION

A man dwells in his native valley like a corolla in its calyx, like an acorn in its cup. Here, of course, is all that you love, all that you expect, all that you are. Here is your bride elect, as close to you as she can be got. Here is all the best and all the worst you can imagine.

--Henry David Thoreau

The old Chinese man came to me in a dream.

"Tell the story," he said.

"How can I tell your story when I don't even know who you are?" I replied.

"You know who I am, but that doesn't matter. You have to tell the Story."

"I still don't know what story you're talking about. I don't know what you mean."

"The Story is time, the Story is existence," the old man said. "Go all the way home and you'll find it. Be a writer, be a storyteller."

My alarm rang. I turned it off and rolled back into a fitful sleep. The old man appeared again.

"Be patient and stay with the Story despite its many threads. It weaves an immense fabric. Just remember this, if you imagine redemption for us, we'll imagine redemption for you. "

The dream ended and I struggled in half-sleep. I heard his voice again, "Redemption," followed by the laughter of crows and the loud growl of a bear. The growl awakened me fully.

He'd said to go home. It's not that I didn't want to, but it was complicated. I live in Santa Barbara, a paradise, but I was being asked to go back home. Home is one of the poorest, least educated areas of the state, a place that people flee to get to places like where I now live.

Here has its problems though. People celebrate a glorious past of Mission Santa Barbara and Padre Serra and vaqueros and great ranchos, but the reality is a lot darker. Sometimes I call this place "the land of the lotus eaters."

I was asked to go home. Poverty, addiction, gang wars, and environmental disaster. But, I also knew that rising above the darkness of the San Joaquin Valley, and above its disaster, was the Sierra Nevada.

I wrestled with the old man's words for months and was haunted by them. Why had the old man appeared to me? Over those months I thought I'd occasionally see the old man in a crowd or lurking behind a tree, but I'd never been able to catch up to him. The old man was probably a figment of a mind that needed to touch something deeper than what everyday life afforded me.

I decided to take the old man's advice and head toward home.

I drove north on Highway 101, then headed east from Paso Robles on Highway 46, the hills on either side of the road dotted with orange fiddle-neck and yellow invasive mustard. At James Dean corner – where Dean experienced the interpenetra-tion of things when his Porsche flew over the tip of the Diablo Range at Polonio Pass and sped down the grade into a left-turning Ford – the world suddenly changed. The highway split and I headed eastward on Highway 41, the pale mustard suddenly over-whelmed by the luminous intensity of goldfields, the tiny sunflower the Spanish called, *"si me quieres, no me quieres."* Love me, love me not, the eternal quest for assurance in the temporal vagaries of romance and fate and notions of God.

On the upper reaches of the vernal hills the fire of orange California poppies swept to the ridges with an intensity that threatened to incinerate my mind. The valleys and lower hills were cloaked with the sheen of gold capped by the fire on the peaks. "Hallucinogenic, it's hallucinogenic," I thought, but at the moment this was the world as it was without mushrooms or datura opening the door to another reality. A red-winged blackbird dropped to a fencepost. In that moment some larger mind suddenly trilled through the bird's form, and as it did, I could see a Van Gogh-like figure standing along the road painting a picture of the fiery hills, his brushes dripping with oranges and golds. The painter opened his mouth and as he did the bird trilled the man's plea, a plea for someone or some thing to tell the Story and set him free, to set all things free. I looked away. When I looked back, the painter was gone. I found myself wishing I could paint like that, to capture and glory in the colors, but I only have words and don't really know if they're up to the task.

Further down the road I could see strange animals peer up from where they grazed among the wildflowers. Not cattle, not sheep or goats, but with a sudden shock I recognized pronghorn. I'd never seen them running free before, though they used to run in great herds through these hills and across the San Joaquin Valley below the Sierra foothills where I'd grown up. Suddenly I could hear a voice in my head, a voice that seemed a response to the bird's plea.

This is it. This is what the old man saw when he entered the world. This is how he entered the world.

The pronghorns might have roamed up from the Carrizo Plain at the base of the Temblor Mountains where they'd been reintroduced after being eradicated, a small gesture toward the restoration of things. They roam across the Carrizo Plain along with tule elk in a pastiche of what the San Joaquin Valley used to look like. Temblor, Spanish for earthquake—the San Andreas Fault runs right through the plain.

The highway wound upward through the blazing fields and over the Diablo Range at Cottonwood Pass where the colors became more sedate and demure, as if to say the human system can only comprehend so much. Despite the cessation, my mind still reverberated for hours into the evening. On the backside of the pass, cottonwood trees were pushing bright new leaves.

The road descended from the pass and on across the Kettleman Plain, then over the small climb at the southern end of Reef Ridge only to descend to the plain once again. It was greener than I'd ever seen it, beckoning in ten-thousand verdant shades, the greens a liberation, but I knew that soon it would be brown and dry with tumbleweeds piled against the cattle fences, everything baked in the blast furnace of summer. Things come and go. This had once been a trading route for the Yokuts as they traveled to the coast for shells – abalone, periwinkle, clam.

In the corner of my vision another man, a dark-skinned man, suddenly appeared on horseback riding at great speed. He was riding from the coast, riding in fear for his life as he tried to stay ahead of the soldiers and priests that followed on his trail. He stared in my direction as if he recognized me.

I ascended the last ridge to the top of the Kettleman Hills, and from there the vast San Joaquin Valley opened up. Below me was the Tulare Basin, once a vast sump for all the rivers of the southern Sierra Nevada. The first white man to look over this expanse saw a valley hundreds of miles long and fifty to sixty miles wide. He described it as a labyrinth of lagoons and *tulares* – the reeds, cattails, and tules – the air full of smoke plumes from the myriad campfires of the countless native *rancherias*.

Long before the valley was filled with rivers and lakes and long before the Sierra thrust to the sky to the east, the basin was the Temblor Sea. The ocean pushed through an opening in the coastal range and formed a warm shallow sea where whales and other cetaceans came to give birth. Sea life flourished. Cutting through it all, *cacharodon megladon* swam unchallenged, the sixty foot precursor of the great white shark with triangular, seven-inch razor-sharp teeth. Nothing was safe. In my mind's eye I saw the lord of the deep darkness, the engine of death, circling and rising from the depths. Its teeth are still found beneath the ground.

I stared across the primeval Great Valley. Before my eyes the Sierra began its gradual uplift above the sea. Rivers formed and descended from the mountains to fill the sea with silt. Eventually there was a valley with a lake along its axis lined with tules, oak, cottonwood, bay laurel, wild grape, and willow. Fish and amphibians thrived, millions upon millions of birds nested and bred throughout the tangle of vegetation, the lake a living organism that expanded throughout the reaches of the Story and my mind.

Where the Kaweah River emerged from the granite keep of the Sierra the water divided and divided again and formed a vast delta that flowed into the lake. A valley oak forest – over two hundred square miles – covered the delta land, the oaks interspersed with sycamore along the banks of the streams.

It's all gone now. The lake and its birds and its vegetation are gone, the valley oak forest also gone save a few hundred acres here and there that stick out like single towers above a desert, the only remains of some great ancient civilization.

I drove out across the dry, dusty lakebed, now crisscrossed by straight-line canals in place of the old chaotic growth, and along the banks I spied three different kinds of egrets and an occasional great blue heron. In the peak El Nino years of great rain, when the dams in the mountains can't handle the flow, the lake always tries to return. Hundreds of thousands of flocking waterbirds appear from nowhere to settle on the water as if they'd been waiting in another dimension of time and space for their chance to return.

It is time to return.

So much is gone.

As I drove I found myself holding out a vision of the return, the restoration, something beyond the poverty, the dusty streets, and the drugs and gang warfare of what this great valley had become, a return of trees and lakes and dignity.

This is why he entered the world. He's been waiting.

I saw the ancient life buried beneath the ground and the snow on the peaks. A wind blowing down from the Sierra carried the sound of chanting and singing. It was a mourning song for all that had died and a prayer to the heavens for all that is and can be, a hymn to the mind of us all.

The Story stirred around me across the valley floor, shook off its dust, and then rose toward the sky like a great raven. It flew toward the distant eastern peaks.

Be patient and stay with the many threads. The fabric will weave itself, and space and time will emerge. Let's sing to us all.

THE RAVEN
February 2009

In the deep silence of space, satellites circle amid scattered debris. Most of these satellites are meant to somehow map, measure, and link together the ten-thousand things, for better or for worse. Out toward deep space and on toward the edges of what can be observed, the universe displays the gamut of its form. Suns birth and die amid pulsars, quasars, black holes. Planets circle distant stars. Below the probing satellites, the spinning Earth circles endlessly around its sun, its human inhabitants wary, not accepting of their lot beneath the stars, not accepting of the ten-thousand things. They thrash blindly, fearfully, painfully.

On the other side of the ten-thousand things, on the other side of every point in the fabric of space-time, the Great Mind watches, encompassing everything, observing its own formation through all of us, through the eyes of all life.

When the Great Mind burst into being it had little idea of itself, inchoate, unformed, swimming into existence. As conditions changed, the conditions became always have been. Everything was random probability played out in every instant. What could happen did happen. The Great Mind was impelled to explore itself. Time moved in fits and starts as in every moment endless possibilities played through the Great Mind's circuitry until in an instant one possibility collapsed into the light of being.

In order to proceed, the Great Mind smoothed time, until time had always been that way and the Great Mind existed both in and out of time, observer and observed, both the ten-thousand things and not the ten-thousand things, always moving, moving toward a greater awareness of where it was and where it was going so it could form where it had been.

The Story arose, arises, and will arise, in no particular order.

The raven rode the uplift past the face of the granite dome, rose above the world and began to turn slow meandering circles above the Sierra ridge while she croaked her message into the wind. As she spiraled toward the east, the raven saw the world was still locked in snow and ice. She turned again toward the west. Thousands of feet beneath where she circled the raven made out a movement by the river.

Maybe the figure far below was one of the men she was looking for. The raven pulled out of the uplift and began a descent toward the river.

The old man emerged from a pool at the edge of the river where he had carefully stayed away from the faster current in the middle. The water was snowmelt cold, but his body had adapted after all the many years of daily ritual. Cleanliness was indeed next to godliness in his life. He wasn't obsessive, but he had to daily wash away his memories of the red dust world below the mountains and of his old land across the ocean in order to stay alive.

Too many memories, ancient memories.

He heard the distant cry of the raven carried on the wind and looked up, then nodded in her direction with a slight bow. Something or someone important would be coming.

Off to his left another old man stirred. He lay on a narrow strand of stark white sand cupped in the hollow of a granite slab that tilted gently toward the river. The slab was a confection of shades of reds and rusts with great intrusions of black shot through. Grey and white boulders that had swept down from the higher elevations during high water snowmelt years gathered in pockets along the river where they had been trapped as the water receded. The old men sometimes sat up all the night during these runoffs, the mountains dark around them under the stars, and listened to the boulders growling and crashing against each other in the riverbed and watched as the sparks flew underwater as rock struck rock like flint on steel. The river illuminated itself.

Though her message was delivered, the raven flew lower and watched. The two men were different. The one emerging from the river was Asian, slighter than the man lying on the sand. The man on the sand was darker and rounder, his skin a deep reddish-brown. He too looked up toward the raven and smiled, then greeted his friend emerging from the river. Up canyon, snowcapped Alta Peak jutted above the more immediate tree covered ridges. This terrain had been home for a very long time for the old men, broken by forays to the great valley below.

Slightly upriver from the men, the raven silently glided toward a dying pine that protruded above the surrounding trees and settled on a dead silvered branch. It was still winter in the low mountains, yet some trees were starting to sprout new growth. The raven studied the men's actions, tried to understand what they might need for their ongoing thread in the Story. After an hour the raven took flight, satisfied with her observations.

The raven ascended a few hundred feet as she flew upriver, then curved behind a crumbling granite ridge, her mission complete. The Great Mind had watched through the raven's eyes and now dwelled on the information. The raven flew on, homeward bound.

Upstream in time the fabric shifted, made accommodation. The Story realigned itself.

ENTRY
April 1859

The sun rose in a blinding pulse over the Sierra Nevada Mountains and moved westward across the San Joaquin Valley toward the Diablo Range along the far side of the great valley. The light illuminated the Diablo peaks and began to creep down the eastern flank of the mountains. A few miles from the top the light reached the gnarled base of a two hundred year old coast live oak tree. With the filtered first light a figure stretched and came alert beneath the oak canopy, then struggled momentarily to remember his personal story as he left one world for another.

Wu Jiyan. Yes, that was his name, but he traveled simply as Wu. He'd been walking for several days from San Francisco toward the mountains on the other side of California. He'd heard stories of their remote vastness and hoped to find a refuge, some place to consolidate his being as he had at Jiuhuashan near Nanjing in southern China where he'd lived for the past years.

Wu rarely thought very much about his personal past, a narrative that enfolded far too much pain and tragedy. For a moment though, the images rolled before his eyes as if his life was ending. Perhaps it was. The images reminded him of why he was there. San Francisco had been just another port city full of white men and a great number of his own people desperate to make money. It was not greatly different than Shanghai.

"Just more of the red dust world," Wu thought.

But, the vista here as he awoke was something he'd never seen before, a view it seemed from a sacred land.

He'd arrived to his sleeping spot late at night under the full moon and so had no inkling of his surroundings, no sense of the topography that stretched to the eastern horizon. When he looked over the vast valley before him, he saw gold, a land of shimmering, sparkling gold lit with flames of orange that stretched to the distant horizon and the high eastern mountains under the new rising sun. Wu was overwhelmed, his mind humbled that he could see such a sight in his lifetime. It seemed like this golden place should be the land of the immortals.

Wu's mind jolted for a moment at the unexpected impact of seeing this new land in the morning light and more images from his old life rolled through his mind. He was a learned man, a civil servant in the vast bureaucracy of the Qing Dynasty and had learned to speak English in order to deal with the hated, unwashed British invaders of his homeland. He was forced to negotiate with the British East India Company when they'd taken to growing opium in India and begun selling it to his countrymen by armed force. His mind touched on the wars and violence that had propelled him here to this place beneath the oak tree – the Opium Wars and the rebellion of the Taiping under the half-mad Hong Xiuquan who thought he was Jesus's younger brother – but he didn't want to dwell on it. Tens of millions had died of war, disease, or starvation and now awaited their fate in the hell called Feng Du.

The light from the golden fields also caused Wu to remember his experience in the cave on Jiuhuashan when Dizang appeared to him the night before the Taiping soldiers came to the mountain and unleashed their bloody carnage. Jiuhuashan was the sacred mountain dedicated to Dizang, the bodhisattva whose life's work was to transform and free all those in hell. The mountain was covered with his caves and temples.

The area was a range of craggy stone peaks that rose higher and higher across the horizon. The peaks resembled the jagged spine of a reposing dragon and had inspired a myth as to how the dragon had fallen from the sky. Others saw the peaks as unfurling lotus blossoms and gave it the name "Nine Flower Mountain."

The entrance to Wu's cave was difficult to find, hidden as it was off the narrow trail up the mountain. The entrance was no more than a slit, a vaginal opening to an inner world that one had to enter sideways with a bit of contortion. Inside a stairway led downward in a descent that was dark at any time of the day. One could either carry a torch or trust his or her feet to memorize every stone along the way. At the foot of the stairs a gently tilting slab of stone formed a great room that opened to the sky above. An opening in the wall led to a small balcony of rock suspended high on the sheer stone face that overlooked the valley far below.

The memory of his encounter with Dizang in the cave was indelibly burned into his mind and the experience now unfolded with a renewed intensity. He was once again meditating during the night at the exact moment Dizang suddenly appeared before him in the darkness.

"The Taiping are coming tonight," the bodhisattva told him. "They'll search every cave and if they find you here they'll destroy the vessel of your body."

Wu was overwhelmed when he recognized the figure standing in front of him. Why would Dizang appear to him? Wu was honored and humbled by the appearance, but he was really neither strictly a Buddhist nor a Daoist. He was simply a layman who lived in the everyday world where Daoism, Buddhism, and Confucianism converged together, where myths and stories merged and pure doctrine was of little matter. There were probably many Buddhist masters on the mountain who wished for such an encounter and were far more worthy.

Wu didn't consider himself a master, or even necessarily worthy, just a diligent human being who'd arrived in the cave through a series of fateful events. As a learned man he'd studied the spiritual disciplines from his scholar's point of view and had his own personal meditation practice. He'd also studied herbs and martial arts. All this though, was nothing compared to the extreme dedication shown by the ascetics living here on Jiuhuashan.

Fate had led him to Nanjing where he'd lived for several years. When the Taiping overran the city they'd killed 30,000 government soldiers and then forced everyone else to convert to their version of Christianity on pain of death. Wu had watched from hiding as people died before his eyes, by gun and by sword. He'd managed to escape to Jiuhuashan and sought shelter as a monk, but now after his years of living safely on the mountain, the Taiping soldiers of the Heavenly Kingdom were now poised to storm the great mountain itself.

As Wu watched the figure of Dizang move toward him, the bodhisattva again spoke to him.

"Times have changed. More is needed and there's yet more to understand. You must go beyond Buddha, go beyond Lao-Tsu."

Wu was confused by the very notion.

"How can I go beyond these venerable ones?" Wu asked. "How can this be possible?"

"You must go now and sail far across the Eastern Ocean," replied Dizang. "When you get there you must find mountains greater than these. You'll know them when you see them and you'll find what you need and who you need."

"Why me?" Wu started to ask.

"Never ask 'Why me?' It simply is. Someone calls you there, someone cries out to you, someone needs you there to help free them from their hell. What you find in those mountains can free him and so free yourself. It's possible that many others can be freed by the merits of your act."

With those final words, Dizang stepped forward into the region of time and space that was both Wu and the story of Wu, entangling their beings, and disappeared.

Wu's mind returned to the present and the vista before him. He carried few provisions, but he didn't require much in the way of food. For the moment he carried only tea, bread, a canteen for water, and a few utensils. He started a small fire to heat water and prepared a cup of tea. After his small breakfast he'd be ready to continue walking down toward the golden fields and on to the great eastern mountains where the new sun rose.

JR
February 2009

It was Sunday morning coming down. JR pulled himself out of bed and into the shower hoping the water would not only wash away yesterday's dust from his body, but would also do something for his mind. Lately he'd been trying to avoid drinking too much, but things seemed to be building up to a point where he couldn't handle it much anymore. Just too many goddamn things.

He let the water wash over his body and for a few moments the muscles of his back and neck relaxed as his mind suddenly stopped thinking of all the goddamn things. When he got out of the shower he caught a glimpse of himself in a corner of the mirror that wasn't covered by steam. His face was red from being out all day yesterday on horseback above Dry Creek trying to collect cattle spread over thousands of acres of steep terrain. He'd had to search from the sycamores down by the creek and on up through the blue oak and manzanita while skirting the dense thickets of poison oak. He'd tried to hide himself from the sun as much as he could under a broad straw hat, but it hadn't been enough.

JR looked again in the mirror and at his red skin framed by his red beard and hair. Not the best genetic heritage for a life on horseback, but it was all he had. Many's the time he'd cursed his redness. He was an Okie and his granddaddy had come to the area below these Sierra foothills back in the dustbowl days. The Okie boys had hung together in school. They'd call each other peckerwood or pecker in ways that could be either affection or derision, like folks in the inner city call each other nigger. JR got called Pecker a lot because of his red hair and it mostly wasn't affection. He hated the nickname, in large part because when his daddy was drunk he'd call JR a "goddamn dumb peckerwood."

JR had been born down on the flatland after his daddy had come back from Vietnam. He'd come back all fucked up in the head and JR had no memory of anything other than that. His daddy was either drinking or being a victim of society or a victim of unseen forces beyond anything JR could possibly do to help until he'd finally up and killed himself. Yet, JR was always, in one way or another, trying to help his daddy to be well, even as the phrase "goddamn dumb peckerwood" echoed through his mind.

Neither of his parents had red hair and JR could still hear his daddy's voice sometimes yelling at his mama when he was drunk.

"That goddamn dumb peckerwood cain't possibly be my son. You musta gone out and fucked someone else."

When his daddy would lie drunk on the couch, though, with his balls hanging out of his shorts, JR knew where he came from. When his daddy called out for another drink, JR would pour him one.

JR pulled on a clean shirt and a pair of old jeans. In the corner was a pair of torn dust-covered jeans next to a pair of old working cowboy boots with spurs, nearly knee high, that he wore with his jeans tucked into them. He grabbed at his straw hat, put it on his head and adjusted it in the mirror. If he'd thought much about it he'd have realized he looked a bit like Vincent Van Gogh headed out to paint. But, that thought was far from his mind. He just knew he was feeling insane again.

JR stepped out the door and headed toward his old truck. He was staying in a mobile home on the ranch where he worked. Though he wanted to buy some land for himself, he didn't know how he was ever going to do it. This cattle and cowboy thing was just downright crazy anymore. The Dry Creek valley had supported more Wukchumne in the old days than it could now support ranchers spread over their huge ranches. The calves that JR brought in from the hills were sold to flatland feedlots for a pittance where they were enclosed belly-to-belly, butt-to-butt in small enclosures and fattened and marbled for the market with drug-laced feed. When the dairy farmers were in a pinch, they'd dump old used-up cows on the meat market, hormone and antibiotic laden, to make fast food burgers. Either way, the cows spent a good part of their lives standing up to their knees in their own shit. JR hated that this was how his work ended up, but he couldn't change how things were. He saw little honor in the way the animals met their fate, the end of their days on the planet. Now, it seemed, being a rancher or cowboy was more a lifestyle choice and vow of poverty than making any economic sense. It was about the only life he knew though, hard work and honest.

He did know another way of life, but he didn't like to think of it much. Like his daddy he spent his time as a soldier. Been to Iraq, but he'd never been much into the holy crusades thing. He only joined the National Guard so he could have some connection to his daddy's memory, but suddenly he was in the middle of a war he didn't understand. Growing up in a fundamentalist church with lots of praying and singing, he never saw many prayers answered, nothing more than random chance, and he certainly prayed a lot for his daddy to wake up, get healed, and maybe love him a bit. He also prayed before missions and sweeps, and prayed over the torn bodies of his friends, to little effect. The only thing praying did was make him feel he was at least doing something instead of just being pushed around by forces beyond his control. But praying also made him angry. It made him feel needy, and he hated feeling needy.

He ended up like his daddy and came home a little fucked up too.

These hills were his solace. When he rode through the granite and the trees he felt free. The smells of the vegetation – the sage and the manzanita, the oak and the sycamore – those smells had the power to lift him out of his suffering. The creeks etched their paths through his mind. Trouble was, all those things were barely working for him anymore and he didn't know why. He found himself wanting more, but had no idea what it was. Seemed there was nothing good in his life that didn't sour on itself.

He got behind the wheel of his truck and headed out the driveway toward the main road, a half-mile drive on a gravel road. Behind him he could see Shadequarter Mountain in the rearview mirror blocking any view of the snowcapped Sierra on the other side. Once on the main road toward Badger he passed a few more ranches until he came to the cafe that sat in the fork of the Y where the road split. It was an old ramshackle bar and café built during

Prohibition to front illicit booze sales, a natural sort of place for the weekend Harleys to park.

He headed through the door and took a seat at one of the bar stools, then looked around the room with a half smile as he made his greetings.

He caught the waitress's eye.

He was tempted to order a drink for hair of the dog purposes, but stopped himself. He was trying desperately to not go down that road.

The waitress came over.

"Whatcha want, Hon? Need a menu?"

It was a joke of sorts because the place had no menu. You just ordered breakfast and whatever the cook fixed for the morning was what you got. The waitress shouted out "One more!" in the direction of the stove, then turned back to tease JR again. Somewhere in ancient history they'd had a thing, but it didn't matter so much anymore. It all came down to teasing and banter and sliding on by each other hardly touching.

JR waited a long time. It certainly wasn't a fast food place and the cook had a way of taking her sweet-assed time. It didn't matter a whole lot though. He wasn't in any hurry and it was the nature of life in these parts.

When the waitress came back she carried two plates, one with eggs and home fries, the other with a slab of ham nearly the size of the plate. As he set to eating, the door opened behind him and two young couples entered. They were at most in their early twenties and bore the signs of their own hard night of drinking and carrying on. They sat at a four-top behind him where their conversation carried to him whether he wanted to hear or not. The girls were mascara-ed up with the look of participants on some TV reality show, their hair tousled. JR preferred his women a little less blatant, a little less high-maintenance. The girls ordered Bloody Marys in their own effort to "eat some of the hair of the dog that bit them," as their boyfriends made jokes about it.

As the boys laughed, one of them suddenly said, "You know I don't understand something. How is it you girls get up this morning and spend an hour fixin' yer hair just so's to make it look like you just got fucked?"

JR didn't hear the response. Maybe it was the this-is-what-life-is shallowness of it and he was not a shallow man despite his circumstances. The conversation had managed to push him over some kind of edge, which he was halfway over anyway. He thought of Maria again for a moment. It'd been over a year-and-a-half since she left without a word, and he still wondered at times what'd happened. For a moment things had seemed a bit more real than usual, then it was over. More things souring.

Maria's face welled up in his mind and he remembered the feel of her body as if she were actually there in the bar pressed close against him. The image and sensation abandoned him as he glanced back at the two couples.

It wasn't just her though. It was everything. What did it all mean? He was tired of his sad-ass cowboy economics and he was tired of looking to get laid. He was tired of being a goddamn dumb peckerwood and he wanted more. He wished somebody could give a rat's ass about his condition, could just hear him, but that was out of the question.

He pushed away his half-eaten breakfast and motioned the waitress back over.

"Yeah, Hon?"

"Take that drink now."

THE RECONCILED AND
THE DAMNED
1766

The Convent of Santo Domingo in Mallorca rippled through the priest's memory. He was standing before a series of paintings that haunted him, had always haunted him since he first saw them as a child. Along the wall above his head were the faces of those who'd lived and those who'd died, the reconciled and those condemned, damned for eternity in the fires of God's judgment. Those who were reconciled with the Church and with God wore the diagonals of St. Andrew's cross and held in their hands a green candle of redemption and salvation, while those consigned to burning and to Hell wore hoods and robes, flames and demons painted across them to proclaim their burning judgment and their fate in the pit of Hell. When he looked closely at the paintings, the priest could almost smell the burning flesh and hear the cries of torment. The condemned in the paintings were the crypto-Jews, the ones who'd been burned for professing to be something they weren't. They'd called themselves Christians even while they still followed the Law of Moses, sinfully ignoring the fact that Jesus had come to correct their sins, the errors of their way. In the paintings, thirty-seven hooded figures wore the flames and the demons to proclaim their fates in the holy, righteous fires of God.

When he first saw the paintings as a child, a knot of fear had formed in his stomach. Though the people in the paintings had died a little more than twenty years before he was born, the island still spoke of them in hushed dark whispers that were warnings to anyone who doubted the power of the one true God in this world. Over thirty thousand people had come to watch the burnings, the images still seared in their collective memory and passed on in stories. Children could overhear their parents talking of the fires and the burning bodies and the smell and the screams. That, or the children found themselves threatened with the same dark fate for their own sinful thoughts and transgressions.

The knot in his stomach spoke to the priest in a voice he could never forget and it chastised him for his inadequacy. He'd had questions about the real nature of human life and he'd had doubts about his beliefs, but he couldn't allow anyone to see them, couldn't let them know that he might not be what he professed to be. His thoughts, his questions, his turbulent doubts were a chaos that needed to be set straight for the sake of his immortal soul. He needed surety and he knew at the heart of his chaos was a central hidden shortcoming—an impurity, falsehood, or sin that was the root of all shortcomings—and that if he could find it and root or cut it out he would know God's grace. He would strip away his own flesh with great zeal to find and expose the sin if he had to, do whatever it took to avoid the burning chaos of questions and the burning flames of judgment.

He'd often returned to meditate on the paintings during the time he lived as a priest nearby. Something hid behind the faces of the damned in the paintings, something so terrifying it made him cringe and fall upon his prayers to keep the loss and emptiness at bay. The faces of the hell-bound circled through his mind and kept him focused on his holy task and mission.

Junipero Serra heard the door open behind him and returned to the present. The guard brought the accused before him. He had God's work to do—judgments to make and a faith to keep pure.

BAD AIR
1833

The Trapper and his men set up camp along the Feather River in Northern California. They all worked for the Hudson's Bay Company up in Fort Vancouver and were under orders to trap as many fur-bearing animals as they could. In fact, they were to strip the landscape of as much animal life as possible. The company didn't want any form of wealth left behind, animal or not, to attract the westward thrusting greed of the Americans.

The Hudson's Bay men had been traveling for over nine months and many of them were sick. The Trapper himself was beginning to feel the fever. When they'd left Fort Vancouver, everyone in the region had been sick, but the Trapper had attributed the fevers to the moist climate and the air of the dark, dank forests of the north. He felt that if he could just get his men further south into a better climate the fevers would stop. Now they were here along the Feather River where the summer climate was hot, humid and buggy. The mosquitoes were an eternal torment that seemed a product of the devil himself.

The group had passed through the area back during the winter and encountered many villages of natives, but strangely, on return, the villages were empty or had completely disappeared. The Trapper was puzzled. He wondered if his mind was playing tricks on him and if all the Indians had really existed at all. Maybe he'd hallucinated their existence, or maybe they were still here and he just couldn't see them.

The Trapper had to post guards at night around his livestock since the few remaining natives constantly tried to steal the horses, probably for food. This morning he'd found that five horses had been stolen despite all his efforts.

"Goddamn Indians," he muttered to himself and looked around the landscape. Maybe they were still here disguised as tules and trees and dirt. Maybe even water.

While his days were hot and damnable, his nights were even worse. His dreams were feverish and he soaked his blankets with sweat, so that by morning's light he felt as if he'd never slept at all. His dreams were chaotic, and crowded by the faces of dark and dirty native people who buzzed like flying insects and tried to bite him. They incessantly pushed at him from all directions and chased him along the rivers, trying to force him into the sea. He covered himself in beaver and otter skins that he'd taken from the rivers and tried to keep the insect people at bay, but his actions seemed only to arouse more of the devilishly angry buzzing and biting. The insect people made their way under the pelts and he could feel them on his own skin poking, probing, biting. He could still feel them when he awoke.

Many of the Hudson's Bay men were incapacitated by the fever and the Trapper didn't know when they'd be able to break camp and move back northward to Fort Vancouver. By now the cool climate to the north seemed like a respite compared to the hell in which he now had to live. He didn't understand what strange vapors could be arising from this landscape, polluting the air, and making everyone so deathly ill.

The Trapper's heart pumped overtime in response to the constant stress of survival in the alien landscape. With each heartbeat his blood pulsed and carried tiny plasmodium parasites coursing through his body and the buzzing anopheles mosquitoes attacked and sucked at his blood, then carried the parasites away far and wide. The Trapper suffered at the center of concentric circles of suffering that rippled for hundreds of miles away from him and his men. The anopheles mosquitoes had never encountered the plasmodium before – were perfect virginal hosts – biting, sucking, swarming, they rode the crests outward on the circles of suffering and downward through the circles of hell. The Wintun, Yokuts, and other tribes along the waterways of the valley dropped like flies, more virgins sacrificed to the demon disease. They died so fast that the Yokuts could no longer keep up with their cremation and their rituals, had to push the bodies into pits without the mourning time of the *Lonewis*, had no time to properly dance and sing the dead toward *Tihpiknits Pahn*, the land of the dead. It was the Great Dying. The surviving Yokuts moved into the hills and abandoned the rivers, marshes, and lakes of the Great Valley for years.

Finally in the autumn, the Trapper and his men began to pack and make their way back to Fort Vancouver. They still suffered intermittently from the fevers, but no one had died. The Trapper continued to write in his journal, speculating about the mysterious disappearance of the natives and of how the landscape could become so suddenly stripped and denuded of human life.

"Mal aria." Bad air.

Elements of Being i

Fear narrows the gate of the mind and we believe what we're told. How does the Great Mind pass through that? We get ripped asunder, and fear works to narrow the gate even more. Such is the nature of politics, religion, and greed.

Wu Jiyan

FOUR CREEKS
March 1850

John Woods finally allowed himself to pause and look around intently at his new surroundings. Everywhere he looked there were trees – trees and creeks. He'd spent days on the road from Los Angeles. Once he and his sixteen companions had crossed over the mountains north of Los Angeles, they'd been confronted by a vast, nearly treeless plain as they hugged to a route along the foot of the towering Sierra Nevada. The only exception was when they crossed the rivers that poured out of the mountains. After such taxing barrenness it was a relief to reach this paradise where they found themselves in a dense oak forest so thick with growth – grapevines trailing sixty feet from the tops of the trees – that it seemed a tropical jungle. The forest covered hundreds of square miles along the delta of the river. The Spanish had called the river the San Gabriel, but the new settlers who traveled through the region simply called the area Four Creeks – though there were many more creeks, creeks that seemed to keep dividing without measure as they flowed out into the delta and the valley.

The road they'd just traveled was the only wagon trail from Los Angeles to Stockton and the men had been sent to bridge the rivers along the way. In May or June the river in front of them would be a torrent of snowmelt water from the high peaks of the Sierra Nevada forty or fifty miles to the east, but for the moment the flow was low enough for them to work.

John Woods was a Pike – that was what settlers from his home state of Missouri were called. So many of the westward moving settlers came from Pike County, Missouri, that later just about any immigrant from the South was called a Pike. In the South the Pikes had no home, in fact had been rootless and landless. Being rootless and landless they were also mostly uneducated, cut off from the grace of life by poverty and homelessness, a caste of untouchables existing with less than the black slaves they abhorred.

The Pikes had nothing and were nobody, desperately wanted something in order to be somebody. When they reached the last edge of America, it was also their last chance to have that something, to claim land and be that somebody. There was nothing they'd let get in the way, nothing they wouldn't do to anyone standing in the way.

Back in Missouri, Woods had come from a large family of nine kids. His pa had three kids, all boys, with his first wife. She'd died in childbirth leaving the forty-year-old widower with the three young boys. He'd looked around frantically until he found a family with a sixteen-year-old girl available and made a hurried deal with her parents to marry her, though she'd had a girl's crush on a boy her own age. Reluctantly, she'd been forced to move in with Wood's dad and take care of his boys and his sexual needs. Once when his pa was drunk and his ma needed to talk to someone, she told Woods how she hated wrestling with his pa's old smelly body, but she had to, she was obliged to do those things. It was more than Woods wanted to hear, his ma's words making him feel unwanted like he was a child of rape. She gave his pa six more kids, including him. Things went on and on like that until the old man got himself knifed to death in a drunken argument over a game of cards. Woods was beat by his pa so many times he couldn't keep count and his stepbrothers tormented him no end – a few times they'd even taken to making Woods endure sex things that he didn't even want to think about. Sometime after his dad died, the sixteen-year-old Woods ran away from home and never returned. He didn't like to stop and reflect too much, because if he did the memories would start to rush in and begin to cut him to shreds like whirling, gleaming knife blades. He just kept himself moving further westward ahead of the memories and toward a dream of having something of his own.

Woods stopped his work on the new bridge to survey his new surroundings. As his eyes scanned the forest around him he decided to take an even longer break. The work party had camped within a few miles of a local Indian village upstream. The tribe was called the Kaweah or Gaweah or Gawia, some such thing. The heathens had no way to write their name anyway, so there was no way of knowing what was proper. All Woods knew as he looked around was that he wanted a piece of this land. It was beyond what he could have hoped for back in Missouri. With this water and these trees he could raise hogs, fatten them on the all the free acorns littering the ground throughout the forest. The ground was a rich floodplain of silt and he knew if he cleared a few acres he could grow most anything he wanted, could build a cabin with the oak trees he cut down. As he daydreamed he gave little or no thought to the Kaweah village upstream. They were less than him and if they were less than what he was, then surely they were only animals, and God's intent for animals was for them to be used or hunted down. He knew what he wanted.

The evening before the work party was to head north to Mariposa, Woods decided to take a walk out along the river. He looked up to the patches of stars that appeared through breaks in the oak canopy and heard a few owls in the distance. Once in a great while he could allow himself to take momentary pleasure in such things.

After walking for fifteen or twenty minutes he heard a sound. He listened closely. Somewhere to his left footsteps sounded behind one of the giant valley oaks and he turned in the direction.

"Who's there?"

A human form stepped from behind the tree as Woods reached for his knife.

"Que pasa?" the figure said.

Woods peered closely at the figure in the darkness. It wasn't one of the Indians and it wasn't one of his companions either. The figure was large, dark-skinned, heavily bearded.

"Speak English," Woods told the man. "This is American land now."

"Ah, yes," the figure replied. "It's hard to keep track of these things. Anyway, relax. You know who I am.

"I can see you want this land, and you can have it if you really want it badly enough. How much you willing to pay?"

Woods was shocked. He'd told no one about his plans and he damn well didn't want to beat to this prize. He studied the stranger as he struggled with what to say.

"Where are you from? Who are you? How can you own all this?"

"I live across the river in a place you can't see from here," the dark figure replied.

"If you're willing to sell the land, then what're you asking for it?" said Woods.

The dark form began to list his terms for the transaction.

"If you want to totally own the land and do with it as you please, then you have to give up your sense of beauty to do it. You can't appreciate the stars anymore, not even a tree. Not for more than a split second. If you allow yourself to really see these things you'll feel remorse and guilt at all you've done and will do, and the pain of that remorse and the pain of your sorrow will be more than you can bear. The fear of that pain will bind you to me."

Woods couldn't imagine anything more painful than his life back in Missouri with having nothing and being nothing. Damn, he knew he'd give about anything to be able to live somewhere with nobody telling him what to do. It was the only chance he possibly had for a slight sense of meaning and immortality, even for a moment.

"Is there anything else to this deal?" Woods asked.

"Your world will have no depth, only surfaces of black and white. You'll never feel the ecstasy of color and form and you'll never be able to see the world beneath this world – see, sense, or feel the things that bleed at your hand. This is the price of absolute ownership."

Woods' moments of color and depth had been few and far between over the extent of his life. What the stranger offered seemed a small price to pay for the land and he found no abiding merit in anything he'd been to date.

"This deal is not only for you, but binds on everyone that follows after you wanting absolute ownership of this place. The only way out of the deal is to sense things for far too long and to make your way through the unbearable infinity of guilt, pain, and remorse."

Woods woke from his reverie and found himself at the beginning of his walk. He continued along the river again and once more had the same conversation and made the same deal. He woke up again. In his dreams that night, Woods walked the land with the stranger at his side, surveying the full extent of his new holdings.

In the village nearby, the chief of the Kaweah tossed in his sleep, then abruptly woke and sat up with a start as if the world was ending.

FOUR CREEKS, PART 2
March 1850

Francisco awoke from his troubled dream and looked around to orient himself. He'd lived so many lives in his lifetime that he sometimes had to stop and recognize where he was. He'd been born on the other side of the Great Valley, on the other side of the lake, *Ton Tachi*, in its center. He was a Yokuts, but he could no longer even remember the name of his village. He remembered pieces of his childhood there, occasional sharp images of life along the shores, of vast expanses of tules and the sounds of water birds whose numbers had overwhelmed his young mind, so many birds that at times they seemed to completely carpet the lake. Remembering the images though, always brought back the pain.

A padre had come with the Spanish cavalry when Francisco was a child and asked to meet with all the people of his village. At the meeting the padre told them of his god and the beautiful life at the mission where he lived. He explained to them that the *Indios* lived in sin and degradation.

"You will burn in a great fire for eternity when you die," the padre told them. "But, I can save you from the fire. Return with me to the mission and follow Jesus and your life after you die will be as good as life at the mission."

The elders talked among themselves for a few minutes and refused. How could life along the lake with its bounty of food be a sin or be a punishment? The padre pressed the issue until an argument arose and then violence. He couldn't take no for an answer when it came to saving their immortal souls.

Sometime during the tumult the cavalry started firing their guns and slashing about with their sabers. They mounted their horses and chased down the elders with their gleaming blades. Francisco's father was cut down before his eyes while his mother ran into the tules and willows. The Spanish gathered as many children as they could during the fight, then forced Francisco and the other children to stand in a line between two horses while a *reata* was stretched from one saddle horn to another. The children were forced to place their right hands around the rawhide rope, one behind the other, their thumbs lashed to the reata with a strip of wet rawhide that dried tight in the heat of the direct sun. When the sun had done its work, they were marched off to the mission and salvation.

While Francisco mulled his dream he looked down at his thumb. It was still deformed after all the many years, a constant reminder. He'd been taken to Mission San Luis Obispo de Tolosa over the old trade route between the Yokuts and the Chumash. Francisco could remember how his family had prized the abalone shell and other treasures from the ocean. The shells represented an entirely different world than he knew. It was said that the spirits of the dead departed in the direction of the setting sun, in the direction of the ocean from which the shells came.

The mission was where he was given his name. He chafed at life in the mission – the forced labor and forced prayer to their strange god that either loved or hated him depending on what the padres had to say for the day, or whether they were angry themselves, or wanted to manipulate him into doing something. He didn't understand these whims of their creator – in fact he resented them. When Francisco became part of the mission he'd become property, property of God and property of the padres to do with as they pleased. He could only bide his time until he could get away from the hellhole. Men who tried escaping and were caught found themselves repeatedly flogged, then forced to wear hobbles so they'd remain properly humbled and chastened properties of God.

As Francisco grew older the padres had taken to renting out his labor to surrounding ranchers. On the ranches he was expected to learn to become a vaquero, but one day he witnessed something that assaulted the core of his being. While he was out riding with a group of older vaqueros, they'd encountered a grizzly bear. The Spanish called the area *Canada de los Osos* because it was so thick with the grizzlies and the bears found the cattle herds easy prey. The vaqueros circled the bear with their horses and their ropes, lassoed each of the bear's extremities, then whipped up their frenzied horses in opposite directions. The grizzly bellowed and roared until the rope around its neck stretched taught and silenced the rage while the bear was pulled apart into bloody pieces. The vaqueros celebrated with a whoop and promised themselves liquor for the evening.

The vaqueros motioned for Francisco to join in, but he couldn't. He sat in his saddle for a few minutes in silence, partly for the sake of the bear's spirit and partly out of shock. In his tribe bear medicine was powerful and honored. You didn't randomly kill a grizzly because it might be a shape shifting bear-medicine man out for his walk or out hunting. That particular bear might very well be one of the most important men in your village. The shaman could jump into a pool of water and come out a bear. In order to return to the human world, the bear would jump back into the same water. You didn't kill for the sake of amusement. He couldn't imagine his namesake San Francisco approving such a thing.

Francisco said a prayer for the grizzly's spirit.

Francisco also participated in the cattle round-ups on the plains. The Mexican longhorn cattle were semi-wild or wild, left as they were to forage over the vast unfenced landscapes. There was little market for the tough, rangy beef but their hides were worth a great deal in trade with the Americans. The cattle were herded up and shot on the plains. Or the vaqueros cut the cow's throats and skinned them, leaving their carcasses to rot in the hot California sun, food for the ravens, coyotes, vultures, wolves and bears. During certain times of the year, these parts of the landscape smelled of blood and death like a war zone, especially in the summer heat. It was almost too much for Francisco; that life could be so casually wasted.

Soon after the killing of the bear, Francisco was out working in the stables when one of the soldiers approached him. The soldier was unwashed and drunk, the man more a hired thug than a soldier, the real soldiers having gone back to Spain years before. He was a *mestizo* from down in Baja hired in desperation to help preserve the order of the mission.

"Hey, *pendejo*," the soldier shouted at him. "I've got a huge problem and you, you *pinche* little Indio, you are going to fix it for me."

The soldier pointed toward his crotch and lurched toward Francisco. Francisco tried to push him away.

"I'll tell the padres, you pinche Indio," the man slurred. "I'll tell them you refused to do your job, or maybe I'll just make you a pinche Indio *muerto*."

The smell of the alcohol and the man's odor nearly overwhelmed Francisco. He struck at the soldier with the broom handle in his hand and couldn't stop. Memories flooded Francisco's mind, the memories he'd wanted most to forget, the memories of the fat, bald padre touching him and trying to do unspeakable things. He hated the padre and this drunken man, he hated this place, and he hated Padre Serra for creating the hell in which he had to live.

Finally Francisco forced himself to stop the beating and wept.

He longed for the spirit of the lake.

Francisco quickly gathered a few things in addition to the knife and rifle the man had been carrying, mounted a horse, and fled north toward San Miguel then across the hills toward the east. The man wasn't dead, but he knew they would soon be after him. With any luck he could make it to the lake country ahead of them.

He pictured how his village would look and imagined how it would feel to once again be out on the tule rafts fishing. He wondered if anyone would remember him and whether it was possible that he could once again feel embraced by the web of daily village life. He longed to be called by his real name, though he couldn't remember what it was.

He rode as fast he could across the hills and low mountains toward the lake. When he finally came to the shore of Ton Tachi he searched up and down the shore for his village. He found a few landmarks for orientation, but nowhere was there a sign of his old way of life. The Spanish had erased not only his life, but also the life of the whole village. Any survivors had probably wandered along the shore until they'd been absorbed into other villages. Either that, or they'd died of sickness and starvation. Francisco felt emptier than ever. He couldn't turn back and the way to the east toward the mountains was unknown to him. The only thing he knew for certain was that he couldn't stop, not even to mourn everything he'd lost, everything his village had lost. He had no idea how close his pursuers were and he had no desire to be the property of anyone again, especially the strange Church, or to be at the mercy of the priests and their god.

Francisco continued around the northern edge of the lake and kept moving eastward until he encountered a vast oak forest and a Talumne Yokuts village called Watot Shulul. He approached the village and found a winatun standing in the middle of the trail before him. Francisco dismounted and approached the man. The winatun was one of the village heads, a messenger to the main chief. His job was to question anyone who approached on the trail and either turn them away or conduct them to the chief. Francisco was surprised to find that despite the fact he came from another village and subtribe that he could still understand the language of the Talumne.

"I seek refuge," Francisco told the winatun. "I seek a family and a place to live in peace."

The winatun guided Francisco into the village where he found a place to sleep for the night. The next morning he met with the chief and his council.

"I was raised on the far shore of Ton Tachi in the direction the sun sets and in the direction the dead depart to Tihpiknits Pahn. I was taken by the Spanish as a boy and taken further in the direction of the dead and the setting sun. I have lived as one who is dead until I escaped back in the direction of the living."

The chief and council were moved by his story, but decided he could only stay for two more days before he had to move on. The Spanish priests and troops had been to Watot Shulul several times in the past looking for runaways, deserters, and stolen horses. The soldiers had issued threats. The chief knew there would be far too much trouble if Francisco and the horse were found in the village.

At dawn after the two days, the winatun searched out Francisco.

"In which direction do you choose to go?"

Francisco gestured toward the mountains where the sun was rising above the granite peaks. He was choosing the direction of the living, of new birth. The winatun led Francisco and the horse into the forest where Francisco lost sight of the peaks.

The winatun soon turned back to the village and left Francisco to follow the river through the middle of the forest and toward the unseen mountains. In places he had to dismount and walk his horse because the trails were never meant for a horse and rider, the area too dense with growth and old fallen trees covered in mounds of wild grape. The dark forest was strung with grapevines that hung from the treetops. The oak forest seemed a labyrinth that led to a supernatural world beyond normal being, a world Francisco had never before experienced, even in the mystery of the Church.

Where a few hills began to rise above the canopy of the oak forest, Francisco encountered another winatun from the Kaweah Yokuts.

Francisco repeated his words as before. "I seek refuge. I seek a family and a place to live in peace."

This winatun guided him into the village. It was simply called Kaweah after the tribe.

The Talumne had told Francisco of the Kaweah. The Yokuts' name for the crow was gaw or kaw for the sound the trickster bird made. Weah meant cry or sound, so to the neighboring villages the Kaweah were The Crow Cry people, named for the noisy and quarrelsome nature of the crows. The Yokuts up and down the great valley liked to pride themselves on their calm and peaceful nature and to them the Kaweah were an aberration, the ones that were sure to cause trouble at any gathering of the villages and subtribes.

Francisco and the chief talked for several hours about the situation. Francisco again detailed his story of loss, captivity, and escape back to the living. He didn't change any detail, even though he'd been turned away before. Despite all his losses, his honor and integrity were all he had to rely on. What had happened, had happened, and to change the details to gain favor would dishonor his life.

Francisco did have one gift to offer though. He knew the horse would be an obvious giveaway for any Spanish that came to the area, especially one broken to the saddle, so he offered it to the village.

Finally the chief and the council decided Francisco could stay. They told him that the Spanish rarely came up the river because of the Kaweah's reputation. The village would know well in advance if the Spanish were coming and Francisco could go to the other Kaweah village up in the hills above the point where the river entered the valley.

The Kaweah had no place for horses or for riding in their way of life, so a feast day was declared to hide the evidence. During his days as a vaquero, Francisco had gained a deep affection for the horses he rode across the land and this horse had carried him back to the land of the living. He had to turn his head when the horse was killed. He felt sorrow and he felt regret. It was another sacrifice among many, but at least the people would eat well, no carcass left to rot in the sun amid the carrion birds.

After the decision was made, Francisco stepped away to take in his surroundings. It was clear enough around the village that he could see to the east the snowcapped mountains. He'd never been this close to the great mountains before and they were impossibly high, vast, and full of grandeur. He'd gone nearly as far as he could without entering the imposing peaks and canyons, and he wasn't yet ready for that journey. He was simply grateful for a place to live and intended to return the favor many times over, protect it as best he could. He'd finally found refuge and he was hopeful he'd find a family and his peace.

He still found it strange that in all the fragments of his memories, he could never remember the name his parents gave him.

Francisco pulled himself from his memories of the past. Last night's dream and his abrupt awakening threaded through his mind, even as he moved through the day in the Kaweah village where he was now the chief. His gratitude to the tribe for his refuge and freedom had resulted in many long years of service leading to his chiefdom.

In the dream he was walking along the river in the oak forest near the village. Just as he caught a glimpse of a dark bearded man among the trees, the ground shook with a great violence. The scene shifted with the shaking ground and he was fishing on a tule raft that floated on a dark lake, just as he'd often done as a child. He was surrounded by dense winter fog as he poled the raft through the dense stands of tules near shore. He could feel the cold dense air start to pierce him when he noticed a surging movement in the dark water. A giant triangle broke the surface near him followed by the back of a monstrous fish. He'd seen sharks before back at the great ocean, but this fish was at least fifty feet long. The fear rose in his throat as the shark submerged, then came rushing up from below the raft, the lake suddenly deeper than it could possibly be, the primal beast seeming to erupt from far below the earth. As the roiling lake water became an ocean with massive rolling waves, Francisco saw the great mouth open and dwarf him, the serrated triangular teeth closing around his body. The teeth tore and sliced at his flesh as he woke up.

CITI CALLING
FEBRUARY 2009

JR returned from the café and barely made it through the front door of his trailer before the phone rang. When he picked up the phone, he heard the telltale pause indicating there was a computer on the other end and then a woman's voice.

He cringed.

"Hello, this is Citi calling about the status of your account."

He wasn't on Dry Creek anymore. There was sand everywhere. A bomb exploded directly in front of his Humvee and the world went into a spin.

"Goddamn bloodsuckers," JR thought as he recovered his bearings.

He wanted to scream at the voice, tell it to fuck off, wanted his voice to somehow penetrate to the core of the computer and fry a circuit board. He wanted the machine to somehow know pain, to know what it felt like to be a human being at the mercy of forces beyond his control. It had always been hard to stay ahead of the money game, but even more so now that the idiots on Wall Street had screwed things up after he'd sacrificed for their survival.

He was under attack.

The voice was that of a harpy from hell that pursued him everywhere.

This is Citi calling about your status as a human being. Your credit score says you're a piece of shit and don't deserve to exist.

JR was simply tired of it all. The world came at him in more ways than he could handle. He didn't understand what the world wanted from him and it pressed in on him until it felt like he was going to explode from the overload to his mind and senses. He didn't belong in this world, but he didn't know where he belonged. Something was always reminding him that there wasn't a place for him, that he was unwanted. He'd drink and look to get laid to forget it all, but he didn't want those solutions anymore. But, he didn't know how he'd survive without their solace.

As a child JR had found himself wondering who he really was and where he came from. Where had he existed before he was born, who was he before he was born? These weren't your normal ponderings for someone in a hardscrabble Okie family, at least as far as JR knew. Who was he going to ask? His drunken daddy, his overworked perpetually tired mama, some fool at the school where he was called Pecker?

JR hadn't found the answers to the questions, but

he knew it didn't involve having a perfect credit score. If the geniuses on Wall Street were examples of the ultimate purpose of life, then he might as well shoot himself right now and be damn well done with it. He worked hard and was square in his dealings with people, but hell, that didn't seem to matter so much. JR was a stickler for fair play. That the snake oil salesmen were always coming out on top and pulling the strings of his life made him crazy. Keeping up with the economics of life made him feel like he was being shredded and consumed by a great beast.

This is Citi calling....

The financial stuff, though, was just a can opener to the bigger cans of shit. The stuff from his family life and from what he experienced in Iraq took him over over and transported him to places he didn't want to go. In his life, you either did something about things or shut up. He had no idea what to do about it, so he just shut up.

The effect of the phone call and the cascade of memories was to make JR feel like nothing and he feared that a lot. When he thought of the Wukchumne that used to inhabit the place and how anonymous they were to him, it made him feel hollow. He'd once heard a cowboy poet from down further on Dry Creek read a poem about the Wukchumne and JR had begged a copy. He still had it tacked to a wall.

Still in the Mountains

Before we came, nothing went to waste –
neither time nor words at idle parked
beneath the Valley Oaks – old men

and boys employed as distant silhouettes
beneath great canopies. At the tip
of a long worn hand, each rock had a name.

Along the ridges, every recollection swirled
and passed some seep of water shared
by wild things. And upon a granite slab

of mortar rock beside the Buckeye's sinewed
fingers, rusty leaves dripped as women talked.
Nothing went to waste, not even thought.

JR felt an inexplicable sorrow and loss when he read the poem, but he couldn't let it go for some reason.

He didn't want to go to waste.

He'd heard how the Wukchumne and a bunch of the other Yokuts had a Ghost Dance up the road a long time ago. They were trying to dance their dead back to life. The image of those nameless people doing their futile dance after they'd lost everything left JR feeling empty and made life seem pointless. As for himself, he certainly had nothing, and he felt like he was a ghost who had no capacity to dance at all. He kept moving with the futile hope he'd find something in his life other than pain.

The image of the Ghost Dance made JR wish that someone cared enough to dance him back to life.

JR had listened to all kind of preachers and seen the new-age guys on TV going on about how you have to think the right thoughts and have the right beliefs and then you could have everything you desire, but damn he knew if he'd had everything he desired he'd be a dead man by now. Some things would be good to have, but not everything. He didn't need much, not mansions or fancy suits like the smiley soft TV guys, just a little meaning and enough money to get by, and maybe if he was lucky, a good woman.

JR thought of Maria.

JR knew he had to take a break. He rummaged around and found his old pack, a sleeping bag, some cooking gear, and a little food in the pantry. He'd stop for more food down in Lemon Cove or on up in Three Rivers. He stopped and looked out the window down the canyon toward Dry Creek. It was still midwinter, so the sycamores and blue oaks had no leaves and the willows along the creek were just red sticks. Because things were barren, the landscape appeared open and you could see things you normally couldn't see.

As he went out the door, JR heard the phone ring.

THE TAHNI UISH
December 1850

Francisco was happy when the invaders left the Four Creeks area and headed northward the day after his dream of the great shark. He felt relieved of some great burden of fate and besides, the spirits sometimes just stirred things up for no apparent reason. He had no way of knowing these things with any certainty. He had his duties to perform as chief of the village and so set about his tasks, all the while keeping a one wary eye directed toward the north. The bridge that crossed the river downstream from the village stood as a stark reminder of his recent nocturnal fear and terror.

In the autumn, word came from the north through the various tribes. The white men were returning, and this time they came with even more men and a herd of cattle. Along with the news of the invaders, word also came that the northern tribes had become angry and restless, determined to push the scourge of the white men out of their territories in any way they could. The Yosemite and the Chauchila were preparing to go to war. Francisco mulled the news that came to him, and as he did, he felt waves of fear rise and pulse within his mind and he sensed the presence of some lurking danger beneath those waves. As he looked across the village toward the trees, it seemed like the waves were going to engulf the land. He felt like he had when he was being tied to the reata as a child and led toward the land of the dead. He feared that his peace and purpose among the Kaweah were at an end, that he would be forced to live among the walking dead once again.

On the southbound trail from Mariposa, Woods felt a momentary fleeting pleasure as he rounded the tip of the hills by the river and began to scan for the bridge. He had been away for too long, but he was back at last, ready to claim his piece of the earth. The pleasure ended when he began thinking of all the things he needed to do in order to fully own the land and protect his toehold on the frontier. He'd been sent back to build a settlement and to collect tolls at the bridge in an attempt to build an economy where the only money existed in the forms of shells, arrow points, and balls of pigment. The savages didn't even have any use for gold. In return for his effort Woods would be able to claim about as much land as he could.

Woods rode on back to his drovers.

"Push the cattle across the bridge to the south side of the river. We'll make camp and then tomorrow we'll set about looking for building sites."

The cattle were let loose to graze beneath the oaks. With a river on each side and a dense growth of living trees, fallen trees, and mounds of vines in each direction up and down river, the cattle wouldn't go far. They had all the food and water they needed.

The grass away from the riverbanks was parched from the intense summer heat. No water had touched the ground since the creeks had overflowed with the snowmelt and deposited their near annual load of silt throughout the forest in May. The deep watering provided by the flood was enough to sustain the oaks through the drought that was summer and fall in the San Joaquin Valley. Sometimes the droughts were year round and sometimes they lasted for a hundred years.

Francisco sent men to watch the invaders' encampment from a distance. He became alarmed when his men told him the white strangers had laid out the foundations for five buildings. In the past, travelers had just passed through the area and done nothing more than camp, maybe trap, but now it appeared the Americans intended to stay. Francisco's mind turned back to the mission days. He wondered how long it'd be before these white men began to enslave the Kaweah and use them for hard labor. Francisco also wondered if these new settlers served the same god as the Spanish and if they worshipped in the same way. He recoiled at his memories of the dark somber missions, the joyless chanting of prayers, and of people teaching him over and over of his sin and guilt in simply being alive. Francisco couldn't imagine this was what the creator would ask of any free human being and he knew he could never return to that kind of life. He'd rather die and be among the truly dead.

Francisco lived an honorable life, protected his people as best he could from harm, and tried to live in accord with the spirits of the place they inhabited. What was sinful about that? It seemed as if the padres needed to bring in converts to prove themselves worthy to their god. The padres spoke of how Indians in other regions took scalps and what a vile sin and desecration it was, but this bringing in converts seemed like some sort of spiritual scalp taking, a point of pride when they stood before their god and held the scalps aloft. In taking these spiritual scalps, the padres had killed his people and left the people's real selves like bloody carcasses on the ground while their empty lifeless shells went to Mass and did what was asked of them. Francisco pictured the carcasses of the wild cattle left out on the plains after their hides were cut away and he shuddered.

Francisco's men soon reported news of two more disturbing events.

"The white strangers are cutting down the trees!"

The Americans were cutting down the oak trees around the area where they'd made foundations. The Kaweah used fallen oaks for many things, including for their own structures, but they never cut the living trees. The trees provided acorns for food and shade during the long hot summers.

"The white strangers are disturbing the sacred dead!"

The invader's cattle now grazed under a special oak, the sacred oak. At the base of the tree were buried the remains and scattered ashes of many chiefs and *tripne* medicine men – bear shamans, rattlesnake shamans, and other healers – and now this ground was being tromped upon by the strangers' cattle, cattle that left the ground covered in large piles of their shit. Tripne was all that was supernatural and sacred to the people.

Francisco knew he had to do something for the Kaweah, both the living and those that dwelled in Tihpiknits Pahn – the land of the dead. He had to do something for all that was tripne. He sent his winatun to arrange a meeting with the leader of the invaders, John Woods, so he could tell Woods of the sacred ground under the old oak. He could only hope that the man would understand and listen to his pleas. Perhaps some arrangement could be made, but Francisco wasn't sure how it was possible. He could only do what he could for his people. There were many more of the white men to the north with guns who were willing to come and take what they wanted.

Francisco knew some English. He'd had contact with American traders at the mission and learned a bit more of the language from Jedediah Smith when Smith had come through the Four Creeks. There were also other mountain men and trappers who stayed for a while on account of the beaver in the rivers and creeks. The trappers killed far too many beaver, skinned them, and threw away the bodies, but at least they'd moved on.

Between a mixture of pantomimed gestures, broken English, and Spanish to fill the gaps, Francisco tried to make his case.

"*Los muertos*, the dead. Think of the tripne dead, the holy dead."

Woods laughed. He laughed at the frantic, rough gestures. He laughed at the halting fight for words. He laughed at the frustrated savage who seemed near tears.

"Those old bones don't make me no never mind. And, ashes don't mean shit to me. This is my land now and I'll do as I please.

"Now, get on outta here!"

Woods shook his gun in Francisco's direction.

It was all superstitious nonsense to Woods. He wasn't letting any ignorant savages tell him what he could or couldn't do, especially for heathen reasons. Though he was a hard drinking and vulgar man, his religious sensibilities were still shaped by the Southern Baptist Church. He could see these natives were going to eventually be a problem and he'd have to deal with it someday. Probably real soon.

Francisco left the meeting with no idea of how to deal with the invaders, the image of the gaping shark's mouth swimming through his mind. It circled below him and threatened to break through and consume his reality. Back in the village Francisco consulted with the winatuns and the tripne men. Despite their quarrelsome reputation, the Kaweah weren't really warlike, more troublesome mischief-makers like their namesake, the crow or raven, than killer.

At the council meeting in the sweathouse made of branches, bark, and tule mats, Francisco told his dream of the great shark that had risen up from the tule marshes. The council listened closely. When Francisco finished his story, old Yahpahkit the winatun spoke up.

"You must speak with the spirit world again. You have to understand this dream and gain the knowledge that will help us survive.

"You have to go through the *Tahni Uish* once more."

The council quickly agreed.

Tahni was the Yokuts' name for the datura plant, the one the Spaniards called el toloache. The plant grew plentifully along the creeks in the places where there was enough sunlight. The plant had a strange skunky smell, but its large trumpet shaped flowers smelled sweetly in the evening and at night. It took a skilled person to harvest and prepare the plant, to know the correct size, the right light conditions and the proper soil. The differences were a matter of life and death.

The old winatun Yahpahkit was the man with the Tahni power. He knew which plants to approach and which roots to take. His job was to slice the roots and pound them in a sacred mortar made for this one purpose, then brew it all into a strong bitter tea. Normally the ceremony was an initiation for the young men, but the situation was desperate, beyond anything the Kaweah had ever encountered. Revisiting the spirit world promised the only answer.

The council members began to prepare the sweathouse for the ritual of purification. The stones were heated.

Francisco paused before he stepped down into the sweathouse. He looked up and around at his world, at the dry hills behind him, the snow-covered peaks of the mountains, and the oaks along the river next to the village. He wondered how he could possibly protect the immense world around him. The fullness of the world surrounded him and filled him, the familiar fullness of the world he knew so well. After a few moments, the fullness suddenly departed and was replaced by sorrow, a sorrow so great it threatened to engulf his being.

As Francisco pushed aside the hides at the entrance, he also pushed aside the sorrow. He entered to sit and pray. The entrance was closed behind him.

Francisco lost his sense of time as the air became hotter and hotter. When the air was finally so hot he could no longer take it, he bowed to the stones and ran out of the hut to the river where he jumped into the water. He repeated the ritual five more times.

After the sixth cycle, Yapahkit opened the lodge to the cooling air. For six days Francisco lived in the lodge and fasted alone, subsisting only on thin acorn gruel. In the interior half-light, Francisco tried to still his mind in an attempt to keep at bay the memories that threatened to overwhelm him. When he remembered his wife and son, who'd died in the Great Dying seventeen years before, he felt the pain rise in waves. He wondered if he would see them again in Tihpiknits Pahn, the land where Tihpiknits the bird god determined who could cross the river and enter. Francisco hoped that he would be seen as worthy when it was his time to enter. He didn't want to become another rotting log in the river.

At the end of the sixth day old Yahpahkit entered with the tahni in a special polished stone bowl adorned with abalone shell from the coast where Francisco had been captive. Yahpahkit chanted a prayer.

Drink this water for Tuusiut;
Drink this water for that Pamasiut;
Drink this water for that Yuhahait.

He moved the bowl twice toward Francisco. On the third pass Francisco took the bowl, contemplated it for a minute as he silently prayed, then drank it all. It was strong and bitter. When the liquid reached his stomach, he focused every bit of his energy and resolve on keeping the mixture in his gut. His body's impulse was to vomit up the liquid and be done with it all, but it would be an affront to the spirits if he couldn't hold the bitter tea.

Yahpahkit led Francisco outside the lodge and down to the river where they turned and walked silently eastward toward the mountains. When they came to a small clearing by the river in the midst of the willow and wild grape, Yahpahkit pointed to the base of a large oak tree. They embraced for a moment and then Yahpahkit turned back toward the village as Francisco sat down.

Besides being the winatun for the village, Yahpahkit was also Francisco's shaugh-num-ah, his adviser and lifelong counselor, a man now well into his seventies. He'd overseen Francisco's first Tahni Uish, had counseled Francisco through the losses of the Great Dying, and had been the winatun who first brought Francisco into the village. When his family died, Francisco fell into a great darkness from which he thought he'd never emerge, and without Yahpahkit's help, Francisco would never have survived the depths of the void. Yahpahkit convinced Francisco that he had a great responsibility to the surviving people of the tribe. The sense of responsibility gave him purpose and had gradually pulled him from the black hole like a great hand. He still carried his obligation to the people with him. It was his meaning in life.

During Francisco's first Tahni Uish, Yahpahkit hid and watched from further in the forest, but this time Yahpahkit left. Francisco was a grown man now, the chief, and he would have to face his visions and his messengers alone.

Francisco sat with his back to the oak as the day began to end. He could hear the cries of different waterfowl in the distance where they were wintering, and the echoing noise of a woodpecker. Sandhill cranes trumpeted as they landed for the night and on the other side of the river a coyote and its young yipped and howled.

Suddenly Francisco made out the eerie hooting call of *Wahtite*, the burrowing owl, across the river. It was strange. This wasn't Wahtite's home ground. The owl belonged out on the plains where she lived in holes in the ground. Wahtite was a winatun for Tihpiknits and Wahtite always cried out when someone had died or was going to die.

Francisco puzzled about the owl's call and braced himself for the unknown. From the direction where Wahtite called came the the sounds of turbulent water, though the river at this time of year was a lazily flowing stream that waited for the onslaught of snowmelt in late spring. Suddenly the river water washed up over the banks in a wave, and the ground in front of Francisco began to buckle and flow. The giant shark from his dream appeared on the crest of the wave and settled in front of Francisco with its maw open exposing the large triangular teeth. The mouth formed a gaping cave from which two human figures slowly emerged in the dim light and approached his place beneath the oak.

Francisco's pulse started to race as the figures moved toward him and began to make out their features. When the faces became fully apparent his heart leaped outward and his mind cried to the spirits. It was his wife and his son. He hadn't seen them since the Great Dying and now they were here before him in his time of need. He rose with tears of gratitude and called to them, but they didn't respond. He paused and called again, called to tell him them how much he loved them, how much he missed them.

They stood before him unearthly silent, immobile and just out of reach. Francisco felt their presence within him, but he couldn't raise his arms to touch them. As Francisco watched the faces of his loved ones, the spirits of all the Kaweah who had departed and now dwelt in Tihpiknits Pahn surrounded him. His wife and son then stepped apart to reveal two more approaching figures. One was a vaguely human figure with a bird's head and a body covered with long feathers. Francisco knew this was Tihpiknits himself, the gatekeeper to the land of the dead. Next to Tihpiknits, a grizzly bear walked on all fours and slowly approached Francisco. The bear began to speak.

"The time is ending for your people, but not yet for you. Even the time for my own kind is coming to a close, just as with the Kaweah. These things are to be mourned, but can't be changed."

Francisco was torn by the finality of the bear's words.

"How can this be so? What can I do, what ceremony can we perform?" Francisco cried out. "What terrible thing have we done?"

"You have done nothing wrong and there is no ceremony to change these things. There is nothing to do but meet your fate with focus and great dignity," the bear replied. "The reasons for this fate don't lie within this realm of time and living and dying."

Francisco wept for a minute, nearly overwhelmed with his grief.

"We are at the mercy of hungry ravenous beings," the bear continued. "Just as my own people will die so will most of the tree people around you. No arrow can stop the ravenous beings, neither can a gun. These beings who are empty and ravenous must come to understand their hunger and do a mourning dance, must grieve for what they've done. They must find the food that fills them with but a single bite and let it end this great hunger on the spot. They must find their true reason for living on this ground and in this world."

The enormity of the loss nearly crushed Francisco beneath its weight, but he raised himself up and brought his mind back to focus on the grizzly bear in front of him.

"You won't be alone, there'll be another who'll come to you. So that the bear spirit remains, I'll travel with you. You must become the seed of this food that fills with a single bite."

In that moment Francisco became a deep pool of water that opened to a river. He watched in awe as the bear leaped forth toward him, dove into the pool and swam through his currents.

Francisco turned his gaze outward, only to see his wife and son fade from sight as the great shark receded into the river.

WOODSVILLE
December 1850

The morning after the Tahni Uish, Francisco awakened to a cold dense fog that penetrated throughout the forest. It was the first of the great fogs that would descend on the forest for the winter. The fog enshrouded not only the oak forest along the creeks, but filled the entire length of the San Joaquin Valley. Settlers would later call it the tule fog, the Yokut's revenge. The fog was so dense that it seemed to have a palpable life of its own.

Francisco pulled his robe tight about his body and began to make his way along the river toward the village. After a half-mile, he was met by Yahpahkit, who turned and wordlessly fell into stride with Francisco. Together they walked toward home. The forest was silent except for the sounds of a few crows in the treetops, whirring, clicking, and cackling.

At the same moment Francisco and Yahpahkit approached the village, John Woods walked toward the edge of the clearing where he and his men had been cutting down oak trees the day before. The settlers had completed the first cabin and were preparing to start another. They'd worked late the night before and when they'd begun to gather things together as night fell, strange sounds had emanated from upriver. The water in the river pulsed in a wave while the ground shook like an earthquake had struck. The event frightened the men and they hurriedly dropped everything and headed back to a good fire and some whiskey.

As he walked back to where the tools were left, Woods found himself cursing the devilishly thick fog that engulfed him. Yesterday evening's events still unsettled him and he was hung over from the drinking. It was his first winter in California and he'd never seen such thick fog in his life. He found it nearly impossible to navigate familiar places in the simplest of fashion. The fog spooked him and its bone chilling cold made him feel as if the life was being sucked right from his body. The eeriness of the fog also seemed to bring out thoughts and images from his past that Woods wanted desperately to keep buried.

When he neared the cache of tools, Woods heard sounds from behind a nearby tree. He moved quickly around the tree where he found two young Indian boys – only ten, maybe eleven – crouched low in a bush, probably spying. As soon as he spotted the boys, Woods began to worry about his tools nearby and forced the boys to accompany him to where he left them. With relief Woods saw nothing was missing, but the relief was quickly followed by irritation and anger. He felt oppressed by the dense gray fog and the memories it brought. He was tired of even having to deal with these savages anymore with their talk of sacred ground and sacred trees. The image of the stranger appeared in Woods' mind again and he remembered the deal. The stranger smiled at him and watched intently as all parts of the scene unfolded.

"Goddammit," Woods thought to himself. "This is my land. I own it completely."

He wanted to make that point perfectly clear.

He found a length of rope in the tool pile and bound each of the boys, then gagged them. He wasn't going to kill them, but he'd make damn well sure they couldn't create more of their kind. Images of what he'd endured with his stepbrothers spun through his mind as he made quick incisions and castrated the boys like he'd castrated so many cows and sheep in his life. The boys' gagged and muffled screams barely carried into the gray fog. Now they'd never be men.

Woods untied the boys and walked away back toward the cabin. He knew damn well he'd made his point. If the savages wanted to believe in magic, then let their magic fix that.

Soon after Francisco returned, the other wina-tun brought the bloodied and crying boys into the village. Francisco hadn't even had time to tell Yahpahkit of his experience with the bear the night before, and now he was faced with the senseless tragedy that stood before him. No man of honor could allow such things to happen to the young of his tribe. Despite what the bear had told him about the fate of things, Francisco wanted desperately to do something. The offense against the boys was too great an outrage to let go unanswered.

Francisco quickly called together the men of the village and they accompanied him to the place where the white men were staying. They walked westward along the river and then crossed on the bridge the white men had built. In the fog the Kaweah could hear the muffled noises of the white men working and made their way in the direction of the sound.

The settlers looked up in surprise and fear as the Kaweah stepped from the fog around them. Francisco could have killed the white men on the spot, but decided against it in order to honor the bear's warning about the futility of violence. He approached Woods quickly. Francisco didn't want to talk about the atrocities. Speaking about them out loud would make them real again, would be just one more indignity inflicted on the honor of the boys.

He wasn't going to bargain either.

"Leave within ten days," Francisco told Woods. "If you do not, you will die."

He turned and instantly disappeared into the fog with his men.

Woods and his men went on with their business as if nothing had happened and Francisco began to wonder if the Americans really understood the gravity of their situation. The white men still cleared the land and cut more trees for more buildings. The fog hung around for a few more days without relief and then finally lifted. The sight of the winter sun illuminated the forest with hope and kept the white men working. It created a sense of safety that pushed back any threat, real or imagined.

The dawn of the tenth day brought the fog again. With it the old sense of dread descended on the white men. Once the sun was up there was little to denote the passage of time, the disc of the sun unseen behind the fog enshrouding the forest. There were no shadows, only the monotone sameness of the diffuse gray light. Trees only ten feet away sometimes disappeared into the fog as it swirled and thickened. The gloom made the men felt leaden, their will sapped. The hope and bravado they'd cultivated in the sunlight suddenly seemed forlorn and desperate.

The men held a short meeting and decided to hedge their bets. They'd bury their tools in the clearing where they could easily find them later, and then leave. When things settled out they'd return and get back to work. The settlers could always get more men and guns up at the Mariposa. One way or another the situation with these savages would be handled, but they had to move quickly.

Twelve of the men made their way to the clearing to bury the tools.

When he'd first given his warning, Francisco had sent for more men from the other Kaweah village up the river and now they gathered unseen in the fog near where the settlers camped. Francisco watched silently while the settlers buried their tools. He'd really hoped the white men would simply heed his warning and move on. He had no desire to be forced to kill them, but when he watched the Americans burying their tools he knew they'd be back, probably with others, and there would be more and more without end.

Despite the bear's admonition, Francisco felt forced to defend his people and their way of life. He couldn't leave the people who'd adopted him and made him their leader at the mercy of these cruel invaders. Francisco rose in the fog and made the noise of Wahtite, the ground owl that always cries out when someone dies. At the signal, the Kaweah appeared from the shroud of fog and filled the air with arrows – silent, deadly. After the volley the Kaweah moved in quickly to silence any possible outcry or any scream of pain, and made sure there were no survivors. Francisco looked for John Woods among the bodies, but couldn't find him. He gestured for his men and headed for the cabin.

Woods and two other men stood in front of the cabin and it was obvious they hadn't seen or heard a thing. When the fog lifted for a moment, Francisco and his men walked across the open space in front of the cabin and into Woods' view. They keept their weapons out of sight and acted as if nothing was wrong.

Something was indeed wrong, though. Woods could sense it. He moved a few steps toward the cabin, then broke into a run as the air filled with arrows. The men who stood next to him suddenly bristled like porcupines with sticks tipped with stone and obsidian, then fell to the ground. Woods ran into the cabin and barricaded the door.

Woods squinted through a hole in the wall. He was surrounded, but the cabin was filled with the entire cache of weapons and ammunition. If the savages tried to take him he was damn well going to give a good accounting. He fired a few shots in the direction of his attackers, and as the bullets flew past, the Kaweah fell back to decide their strategy.

A half hour passed. When no one else showed up to defend him, Woods knew for certain there would be no help. He was in the fight alone.

Every time the Kaweah advanced, Woods opened fire. He knew he'd killed some of the savages, but they seemed relentless and driven in their pursuit to get at him. Minutes after his ammunition ran out, Woods heard movement on the roof and the sounds of banging and chopping. Before he could respond, the savages came pouring through the roof and engulfed him. When they roughly grabbed him, Woods saw one of the goddamn savages was carrying an axe. He smiled ironically. They'd used one of his own tools to get to him. Woods looked toward the hole in the roof again as the Kaweah carried him out the door. The bearded stranger's face peered at him through the hole – watching, grinning, watching – then disappeared.

Woods yelled toward the hole. "This is my land, goddammit. It's mine."

Francisco ordered Woods lashed to a tree, then walked up to look into Woods' eyes. Francisco was always taken aback by the bearded faces of the settlers, and by the lack of any real expression behind all the hair and dirt. He didn't know what he expected from looking into Woods' eyes, but he had to see if there was a human being inside the shell of a body.

With a start, Francisco saw that the bear had been right about the emptiness. Francisco also saw glowing coals of deep burning anger. The anger appeared to be old, centuries old, and it pervaded the man's spirit. Francisco didn't know whether he was looking at a man or a demon. The combination of the emptiness and the anger was a vacuum that pulled at Francisco's being and tried to bring him spiraling into the man's abyss. Francisco fought to steady himself at the edge of the darkness. He stared into the black void and it seemed to become the cavernous great shark's mouth. Something in the abyss pulled at him again and he recoiled at the memory of being dragged over the serrated triangular teeth.

Francisco pulled back from Woods' face. If this was indeed a demon then it should die. If it was a man, then Francisco might let him live, though he didn't understand how a man could live with such insatiable, unquenchable hollowness. For a moment Francisco felt sorrow for Woods. When Francisco had lost everything, the Kaweah had taken him in and given him back a life, but this man seemed to have nothing that could give him back the fullness of life.

Woods looked at Francisco with stoic silence. He'd be damned if he'd give the savage any sense of victory.

Francisco weighed the possibilities in his mind. He found himself angry at the spirits, angry that they would allow men such as this to torture his people. The Spanish and the Americans had done nothing but take things. Even when they said they were giving they were taking. He wanted the suffering imposed on his people to end.

Francisco drew his knife, the one he had taken from the drunken mestizo soldier long ago. He angrily began to skin the white man like he was a deer or bear. Demons had human skins and were stuffed with tules where their organs should be. He had to know the source of this evil and of this betrayal by the spirits.

Woods remained silent while his skin was being peeled away, but inside he was screaming and cursing at God as his life played through his mind. He'd never had anything in his life, and now that he did, he was being butchered like a pig. He'd been raised in poverty and abuse, and his reward for the hard struggle, his reward for his great effort at simply staying alive, was this flaying. It was surely God's cruel joke. How could God allow something like this to happen, to reward these savages, these animals, more than a Christian white man like him?

In the middle of the flaying Francisco stopped. He heard the bear's voice in his ear telling him again how futile violence would be in combating these demons. He remembered the depth he felt when for a moment he was a deep still pool and the bear dove into the water that he was. Francisco looked deeply into Woods' eyes again and found himself looking at his own face through the white man's eyes. He felt for an instant the pain and the raw torn flesh of the body. The man was not a demon. Francisco remembered the sorrow he'd felt for the man.

Francisco stopped, threw down the knife, and walked away. Behind him one of the young men picked up the knife and made a move to finish the bloody work, but Francisco turned and gestured that it was over.

In the midst of unbearable pain, Woods suddenly found his hands and feet released. He stumbled toward the river to get away, fell into the sand, and didn't move.

EL DEMONIO
1766

Padre Serra entered the room with a limp, a limp he'd had since he first arrived in Mexico over fifteen years before. He was offered a mule to ride from Vera Cruz to Mexico City, but as a declaration of his humility he'd declined the ride as more comfort than he deserved or needed. He'd walked toward the capital and to avoid all distraction, he'd recited the rosary at each step of the journey. A poisonous snake had slipped beneath his pious perception and laid waste to his leg with a single bite.

The padre took a seat at the table and waited for the guard to bring in the accused. When the woman arrived, the padre indicated for the guard to seat her across the table from him. As she took her place, the padre looked the woman over to see what sort of person she might be. She was nervous and afraid, and the fact pleased Padre Serra in a grim fashion. He knew the woman's fear gave him the upper hand and that was exactly the way he wanted it.

The woman was charged with witchcraft, though the padre would neither tell her why she was being investigated, nor if, indeed, there were any charges against her at all. It was a standard tactic of the Holy Office of the Inquisition that he used to extract as large a confession as possible, unconfined by the specifics of any simple charge. Padre Serra was a comisario of the Holy Office in eastern Mexico and it was his duty to get to the bottom of these things, to establish order in the name of the faith.

The padre and the woman were sitting in a dim windowless room located somewhere in the same prison building as her cell, the room lit only by a few flickering candles since the padre preferred the dim light without the intrusion of color. There would be less distraction to his mind and his senses as he tried to ferret out the truth. The dim setting would also disorient the accused. He was confidant in the cold logic of his mind and was sure that if the woman was indeed in league with *El Diablo*, that his mind would be able to penetrate all the deceptions and lies that the woman, in concert with El Diablo, could possibly create. The padre refused to be deceived.

The woman was a mestiza, something the padre viewed with suspicion. These mixed race people sometimes combined the worst of both worlds, especially when it came to religion. Though she might have some Spanish blood, she was probably mostly Indian or African. These mestizos often said they were followers of Jesus and the Church, telling the padres what the fathers wanted to hear – only they still practiced their old ways and used peyote and worshipped their dark pagan gods.

Padre Serra knew these mestizos weren't much different than the crypto-Jews burned in the fires back on Mallorca, the ones who'd falsely claimed a conversion to the teachings of the church. Lies and deceptions, nothing but lies and deceptions. These mestizos represented a threat to the order the padre and the Church were trying to create with the missions he'd established throughout the Sierra Gorda and with his ministry to the Pame Indians.

Not only was being a mestiza a problem, but so was being a woman. Women were weak and easily succumbed to the temptations and wiles of El Diablo. Women couldn't possibly have the strength of will and clarity of mind, like the padre had, when it came time to deal with the fount of evil. It was simply a fact that women were weak-willed and unfocused. The sorcery and witchcraft the *bruja* represented was a product of the devil in his attempts to pervert the Church and its one true vision. Padre Serra couldn't convict her merely on the basis of sorcery though. He had to get her to admit that she'd consorted with El Diablo, that she drew her power from the devil's dark reservoir of malevolent evil.

The woman was dirty and unkempt. She obviously didn't take much care of her body or her soul. She could scarcely sit still in her seat and her eyes flitted about the room, never able to fix her attention totally on the padre.

Probably the devil feeling the impact of God's holy presence, Padre Serra thought to himself.

He knew it would be an easy matter to trap her using her own words. In his hands the padre held a copy of a confession she'd made earlier to the local military but it had never been properly witnessed or notarized, though the woman didn't know he had it.

After he asked the accused if she knew why she'd been arrested, the padre looked directly into her eyes.

"Have you ever made a pact with or had communication with the Devil?"

It was necessary to know this. A true bruja would have to have sold her soul to the Devil.

"No, but it is true that El Diablo has appeared before me several times in the form of a Pame Indian, and other times in the form of a dog, and other times as a cat and other times as an eagle, or as a small lizard or like a snake, or in the form of a Centurion on a black horse with an embroidered saddle."

"Have you ever made a compact or concert with the same Enemy," asked Padre Serra.

"No!"

"What was it the devil said to you, and what did you ask him?"

"He asked for my soul and he said he would give me clothing and support, but I said no."

"Have you ever executed any *hechizos or brujerias?*"

"No!"

Padre Serra halted his questioning and sent the woman back to her cell. His trap was laid. Two days later he directed the guards to bring the woman back into the same interrogation room and seat her in the same place across the table. He read back a transcript of their previous session.

"Did you really say these things to me? Are these true statements?"

"Yes," she replied, "but I am a Christian woman and would never have committed any of the acts you have charged me with. I am not a witch and have never cast an evil spell on anyone."

"Can you deny that on another occasion you gave a sworn declaration admitting to the crimes that you are now charged with by the Inquisition? Because, if you deny having done so, you will be guilty of perjury before God, the Church, and the law."

Padre Serra paused.

"It would be better if you just confessed right now to your terrible crimes."

"I have not committed any crimes. I am a Christian woman."

Padre Serra knew the woman was ensnared. He began to read back her original confession that hadn't been notarized. He read to her how she'd confessed she made a pact with El Diablo a year before, and how she was tricked, the devil winning her soul. After that the devil would go by her side and tell her how to harm the Cristianos. Sometimes she came upon him in the form of a Pame Indian, a coyote, a skunk, or a cat. She slept with him when he was in the form of the Indian and he would enter her, inciting her to wild sexual abandon. She went with the devil when he was in the form of a bat and sucked the blood of little ones who'd died without baptism. She secretly took the Eucharist from her mouth at communion and stuck it under the altar rail so she wouldn't know the taste of Christ's body, and she took bones from the dead for use as a talisman and used peyote in secret ceremonies.

After each clause he read back to her, the padre asked, "Can you hear me? Do you understand me?"

"Yes, I hear and understand."

When the padre first read the confession in private, he'd tried to preserve his equanimity as if he were hearing her speak in the confessional. He found himself reacting though, as another small seed of chaos began to grow and expand in his mind. He found himself transported back to the paintings in the Convent of Santo Domingo and felt again the chaotic fear that had overwhelmed him when he looked into the eyes of the damned. When he read the woman's confession it took all his will power to force the chaos back into the crack in his being and cover it over. Her dark activities were an affront to the order of things, an affront to God's order, and an affront to his need to know definitely where he stood in relationship to that order. More than anything, a life with El Diablo was one of uncertainty followed by eternal punishment, and certainty about one's heavenly salvation was the only thing of consequence in life.

Faced with the threat of perjury, the disheveled woman chose to admit everything. To emphasize the point, the padre repeated the whole process of reading back her confession clause by clause.

"Did you declare that? Did you do that?"

"Yes," she replied wearily, "except I didn't fuck the devil or suck the blood of infants." She was too tired to even be angry.

The admission was enough for the padre. He had what he needed.

Padre Serra summoned the guards to take her back to her cell. With his trap sprung, he could now send her to Mexico City where she'd appear before the Office of the Inquisition.

With his comisario duties completed, the padre reached for his walking stick and hobbled toward the door. Beneath his robe he wore a shirt woven with sharp wires pointed inward toward his body. With each limping movement Padre Serra's muscles pressed his flesh against the shirt. He half-smiled as he felt the wires bite into his flesh, a constant reminder of his dedication to the one true way and the will of the one true God.

BETWEEN WORLDS

Woods felt his body fall into the sand near the river's edge, then suddenly all physical perception ceased. He no longer felt his arms or legs, no longer felt the pressure of his body on the ground, no longer felt a breath. He no longer felt the pain where his skin had been pulled from his body. The absence of pain brought a feeling something like peace, but it wasn't quite the same. A light flickered on the other side of the river, so Woods picked himself up and moved toward the source. He had to find freedom from the suffering he'd endured.

At the river's edge he found a bridge across the deep and smoothly flowing river, but it wasn't the one he'd built. This bridge was too narrow – not near wide enough for a wagon or even a horse to cross. He knew he had to get to the other side and make it to the safety of the light, but when he stepped closer to the river the bridge narrowed even further. He placed a foot on the bridge and it narrowed to the width of a ten-inch log, then narrowed again. Woods wasn't a man to shirk from a challenge and he focused his mind as best he could.

He cautiously stepped out on the log and all sense of the near-peace deserted him.

The memories that flashed through his mind when he was tied to the tree began to return, then amplified to take over his mind. The sum of all the fear and anger he'd felt during his lifetime rose up in a thundering wave and crashed over his being. The onslaught of anguish and terror overwhelmed him just like the savages had in the cabin and he fought to keep his focus and balance. He tried to fight off the wave and the savages, but felt his feet slip and his body fall toward the water.

The moving water became as turbulent his mind and surged around his body. The river tossed him wildly in every direction. He sensed that if he could manage to focus his awareness he'd be able to navigate through the cascade of water and emerge intact. Sharp rocks tore at his body as he tumbled in the river and each grinding, ripping collision reminded him of the flaying he'd just endured. Each memory, each sharp rock in the river, fueled his mounting anger. He cursed at God, he cursed life, and he cursed his existence.

There had to be a way he could focus his mind and get out of the goddamned river, but he couldn't find it.

His angers, beliefs, and lusts mixed with the current and he lost all choice in what happened to him in the turbulent water.

He was overcome by pain. It wasn't a physical sensation of pain, but a pain that pervaded his entire being, something beyond any description he could give. Not only did he feel the agony and suffering he'd endured during his lifetime, but also felt the sum total of the fear and pain he'd inflicted on others.

He tried to concentrate, tried to free himself from the disrupting turbulence of the whitewater and his mind.

The last bit of his will slipped away in the current.

He was surrounded by the presence of others in the river, but it was no solace. As the cohesion of his will broke down, Woods felt the agony of the others in the river wash over him in a yet greater wave of torture. Soon the current of the river slowed and all perception of movement and change stopped. He was stopped, suspended and suffering, in a motionless, timeless eddy like an insect trapped in amber until the Great Mind decided to throw him out into the realm of probability and chance once more.

Elements of Being ii

Who knows the fate of the universe? It carries on waiting for us to join the debate. Dark matter lurks in the folds of space-time – ballast – balancing, righting the ship of existence. It stays the course. The unseen matter awaits guidance, the joining of mind with Great Mind.

Wu Jiyan

NOTHING SPECIAL
February 2009

The two old men sat by the river, a gentle breeze blowing down the canyon. In the peace of the moment, Wu remembered something he read long ago back in China, a poem from Pang-yun. He'd contemplated the poem many times over the years and immersed himself in it.

When the mind is at peace,
the world too is at peace.
Nothing real, nothing absent.

Not holding on to reality,
not getting stuck in the void,
you are neither holy nor wise, just
an ordinary fellow who has completed his work.

Though it was still midwinter, the lower elevations were bathed in the midday sun and the landscape warmed between storms. It sometimes snowed at this level, but it never lasted for long, especially in a La Nina drought year like the present one. Wu simply wore a flannel shirt with worn out khakis, while Francisco also wore a flannel shirt with old loose blue jeans. At the moment it was all they needed. The two laughed and joked a bit as they tried to guess what more the raven had been trying to tell them during the morning.

"Maybe she came to warn us we're getting old," said Wu.

"She's a little late," laughed Francisco. "We were old a long time ago."

Though they knew someone or something was coming, they had no idea of the details. All they could do was wait and see what unfolded from the Great Mind.

The old men had been together nearly 150 years while roaming the foothills and mountains of this small stretch of the Sierra Nevada. They were perplexed by their condition and never thought of themselves as immortals. All they knew was they'd lived for a very long time and left it at that, just two old men who endured by the river and tried to complete their work. Though the old men assumed there was a purpose in it all, the purpose had never become completely manifest or clear. In the meantime the hours and days rolled by, the planet circled the sun, and the two men still had to look after the survival of their bodies. Nothing was for sure, even for "immortals." They still had to pay attention to the details. They slept, they ate, they shit. They studied life and their relationship with it as closely as they could.

The midwinter warmth and the raven's portent for the day caused Wu to close his eyes and remember his first entry into the Great Valley, when he'd descended along the creek and set foot on the valley floor. He found himself walking across the vast plain of flowers that stretched eastward toward the mountains. He was momentarily convinced he'd reached the celestial realm where the deities and immortals dwelled. The colors and forms of the golden realm took him over and impinged so deeply on his senses that it seemed he was living the experience again. As he continued to walk, he encountered great herds of wild horses and rangy longhorn cattle roaming across the landscape, feral animals escaped from the Spanish. The horses always kept a distance, but the cattle seemed angry, as if they retained ancestral memories of some form of abuse at the hands of men. The cattle were more than willing to attack at any provocation.

Wu had to rely on his gift. When he'd escaped down the mountainside at Jiuhuashan, Wu discovered that he'd been given one simple power in his encounter with Dizang, the power to go unnoticed. He'd been able to travel down the mountain trails and around the camps of the Taiping soldiers without being seen. He wasn't invisible, it was simply that he wasn't noticed unless he wanted to be. He traveled all the way down the Yangtze River in this fashion until he was able to catch a ship from Shanghai across the eastern ocean.

All during the days he crossed the flat valley plain, Wu drew upon his power of going unnoticed to get past the herds of angry cattle that otherwise would have trampled him. He'd never been among herds of wild animals before, never been in a vast landscape that was still so undivided and free of human habitation. China was crowded, with every piece of valley floor divided into farms and myriad villages. Even some of the mountains had been stripped of forest and terraced from top to bottom with rice paddies. In this new land things still existed in something closer to their original state. Even the threatening herds of animals couldn't diminish Wu's sense of being in the celestial realm.

As he walked, Wu deeply studied the landscape like it was his own mind. He wanted to understand all the details of his existence in the new golden world. When Wu looked around closely at the ground he'd found that it wasn't a solid carpet of grass with flowers poking through like in a mountain meadow. Rather the grasses grew in wiry bunches interspersed with the golden wildflowers. Sometimes the golden patches gave way to smaller swathes of purple and occasional spots of pink. In looking backward, Wu knew he'd been fortunate to see things in this more primal state. The land had undergone many changes over the years since then. Different grasses covered the landscape now and turned dry and yellow in the summer heat. The flowers now only existed in the hills and had to compete with the dense growth of the new alien grasses.

Wu continued traveling eastward toward the mountains until he came to a river in the middle of the valley that was lined with trees and rushes. After he managed to cross the river, an impulse guided him to turn south. He walked for days until he encountered a vast oak forest that extended toward the east. Just before he arrived at the forest, a brilliant dawn illuminated the snowcapped mountains and the range of peaks was outlined starkly against the sky. Over the previous days the sky had been hazy and cloudy, but on this morning the clarity was overwhelming. For the first time he could see the jagged peaks stretch across the horizon like a saw blade ready to cut through his conceptions about life. The peaks reminded him of a dragon's spine, but these peaks were much higher and far more remote than the peaks of Jiuhuashan. Suddenly he knew without a doubt the mountains in front of him were his destination, that indeed, the jagged peaks on the horizon indicated the place Dizang intended for him to be.

When he came to the oak forest, Wu turned toward the east and followed the rivers toward the mountains. He noticed as he walked upriver how the myriad braiding creeks and rivers began to consolidate until there was only one river descending from the mountains. The river exited the mountains between two hills that stood guard like pillars at a temple. Wu was struck by the sexually fecund nature of the scene. The flanking hills seemed as if they were female thighs giving birth, delivering the life of the river to the valley forest below. He walked through the portals into another world, a world where Francisco waited for him on the other side.

Wu's mind returned to the river and the multi-colored rocks around him. He still found it amazing that he could relive an entire part of his life in an instant. The taste of the colors of the long ago celestial realm lingered in his mind.

Wu's and Francisco's beings had become entangled over their long time together. In response to Wu's time shifting memories, Francisco began to relive his own distant past before they'd met. Something was approaching and it was pulling the memories from deep within his mind. After the massacre, he moved with the remnants of his village to the other Kaweah settlement beyond the portal in the hills. Though the army hadn't hunted him or his men down after the killing of John Woods, life became more difficult along the river on the valley floor. More and more settlers arrived over the years in the company of their animals. The hogs soon ate all the acorns so they'd fatten quickly and in turn were sold to hungry miners. They hogs also tore out the roots the Kaweah prepared for food. The cattle ate the grasses – the clover, the miner's lettuce, and even the wild oats the Spanish had brought. The wild game like the jackrabbits and the pronghorn were deemed nuisances and exterminated. No longer could the Kaweah perform their rabbit drives without trespassing on some farmer or rancher's land.

Francisco hated the hogs. They devastated the earth like manic demons, uprooting everything in their path. They seemed like animal extensions of the voracious American Pike spirit. When the Pikes drove their herds of hogs to the mining camps, many of the animals escaped and roamed wild, attacking unwary people. As soon as the hogs escaped they began to revert to a primitive, survivalist state and took on a fearsome look, almost instantly growing bristles and tusks and becoming the dreaded animals the settlers called "tule rooters."

Worst of all were the Death Riders.

At first Yokuts were allowed to live on the land, but soon the settlers wanted everything. At night, armed groups of settlers, mostly Pikes, arrived at the Yokuts' homes and forcibly gathered everyone together. Those who protested, ran, or were too slow, were shot and left as warnings. The rest were force-marched to the nearest reservation and dumped on the doorstep, after which one of the Death Riders would take over the Yokuts' land.

Francisco and the remnants of the lower village decided to withdraw to the hills to extend their fate. Francisco lived in fear of the Death Riders. Not all the settlers were Death Riders, but the settlers who disapproved of the killing also lived in fear of them. Some of the more benevolent settlers hired the Yokuts as cooks and wranglers, but eventually the Riders would come round and force the natives away.

Francisco couldn't understand why the Yokuts had no rights as human beings. The settlers treated their livestock better than they treated his people. Sometimes the settlers made children with the Yokuts. Didn't that prove they were the same?

In the settler's eyes there was absolutely nothing he could do that was meaningful or right except die. Even the governor of the state they called California spoke of "extermination of the savages" as the only solution. Who could Francisco appeal to? The ways of the spirit world seemed to have little relevance in this mad world of grasping, greedy people. Even if he accepted their religion and their God he could never walk freely in this settler's world. He could never have the land back, not even the smallest piece. Someone would always want it. He could never walk along the creeks in the valley again because he'd be trespassing. Someone would think he was there to steal a cow or pig. They even claimed to own the water.

Francisco really didn't know what sort of people they were. When he thought about it, he was still unnerved by the emptiness he'd seen in John Woods' eyes. He saw that same emptiness in the eyes of many of the settlers. From what Francisco could remember of his days at the mission, their God was supposed to reward believers for a life well lived, yet these people acted as if life had no meaning except for what they could possess. Despite all they'd taken, they'd kill their own to have more.

Francisco regretted killing Woods. The act brought neither peace nor justice to him or the tribe. The boys that Woods mutilated died from the American diseases within a few years anyway, along with over half the remaining tribe. He wondered if the Americans had any capacity for regret or remorse. It seemed something they wanted to avoid at all costs, as if the weight of the remorse would be too much to bear. They spilled new blood to try and wash away the traces of the old deeds and old blood. Maybe the Americans did it with the hope they could deceive their Creator. They thought if they simply believed in their God that all was forgiven, all was right.

Francisco arose each morning with as much dignity as he could muster to face the losses that might rise in his memory. Francisco didn't understand all the ways of the spirits, but he did know that he had to pay attention no matter what happened and that he couldn't pay attention if he fell into fear, anguish, or despair. He had no idea how long they could live in the hills before they'd be forced onto the reservation. He carried forth for the sake of the last of his tribe and he carried forth for the sake of his vision of the bear.

There was supposed to be another, so he waited. At times he felt the bear stir inside his body.

Francisco had waited as patiently for Wu as he could and now the two old men lived and breathed along the river waiting for yet another. The human scale of time seemed of little relevance to the unknown larger purpose. Year in, year out, the snows and sorrows came and went. The river rose and fell, ebbed and flowed, beneath the cycles of the sun and moon. The old men drew energy from the mountains and their friendship sustained them. Their laughter echoed along the rivers.

HOSPITAL ROCK
February 2009

JR drove his battered pickup up the park highway toward Sequoia and felt tired, overwhelmingly tired. He turned into the parking lot next to the highway where the sign said Hospital Rock. He was drawn to the place by some force he didn't understand, but the closer he came, the more his pain and his burden increased. It seemed like something within him wanted to break out, but he was fighting like hell to keep it in place. If it broke out, though, he was afraid he'd no longer be able to function in the world, that he'd be just too damn crazy.

Across the highway the main fork of the Kaweah River flowed between giant boulders creating falls and some deep pools. Around him new bright green leaves on the white buckeye branches seemed to dance suspended in air without visible connection. Though he could intellectually appreciate the beauty to a small degree, he no longer could feel it in his body, could no longer feel the electric visceral response that made his life in the mountains worthwhile. He'd been here before, sometimes with his daddy when he wasn't drinking, a few times with Maria. He could still remember her standing in the pools on Paradise Creek across the main river with her wet skin and the sun dappling across the water. It was good, but it hadn't been enough. He hadn't been enough.

He slowly opened the door and moved from behind the steering wheel. He was wearing his blue jeans and an old shirt that had been repaired in too many places, the shirt a victim of too many encounters with barbed wire and branches.

JR really didn't know what he was seeking. It wasn't Maria, though somehow he knew it had a feeling like her. Though part of him longed to touch her body again, it wasn't a body he was seeking. Even the sexual experience was somehow dimmed for him. It was now more mechanical than ecstatic, as if he were desperately trying to recapture some distant more rapturous moment that no longer existed. He didn't even know if that type of experience was even possible for him anymore.

She always told him he didn't say much to her. Truth was, he didn't have the words for his experience, not only of pain and of suffering, but also of universes that threatened to intrude on him and take away what vestige of self he retained. If he'd said much at all, she'd have thought him crazy. Either that, or she would have been incinerated by the sudden burst of his galaxies of overload.

He was looking for a point of stability, something to keep him on the earth, but no woman had been able to do that. It wasn't fair to ask and the only thing he could take pride in was the fact that he wasn't asking anymore. He now assumed the dimensions of his fate, and that fate resembled some small isolated prison satellite orbiting in the far reaches of distant space, far away from warmth and love and meaning.

He pulled an old backpack from the bed of his truck. It was an old external frame pack given to him by his daddy before he'd killed himself. At the time it seemed the best thing going, but now it was a battered relic with its rigid aluminum exoskeleton. JR strapped it on and headed across the highway toward the river. After crossing the road he stopped before the rock that gave the area its name. At the top was a faded red Indian painting that trailed down the rock face beneath a spreading canopy of live oak. In front of the great granite boulder rested a smaller egg-shaped, lichen-covered rock that stood on end. It seemed like a dragon's egg full of some vast energy to which he was not privy.

He walked by the rock and a flash of blue crossed his vision as a jay flew past, screeching at his intrusion. The only thing he knew was that he was heading upstream and he didn't know if he was coming back. On impulse, he left the keys in the truck as an invitation to anyone who wanted it.

He heard a sound in the distance toward the mountains. On a far ridge he could see snow atop towers of rock that looked like the battlements of a castle. Closer at hand a solitary pine protruded above a canopy of dark-foliaged live oak and, above the pine, a black shape glided high on the wind.

THE BEGINNING

February 2009

The coyote trotted into the clearing with its head high, ears alert, while sniffing the air. His mate followed several feet behind. She'd just become pregnant, but there were still several months of gestation ahead before her two or three pups would be born. For now she still followed her usual cycle of hunting and foraging. In the dense brush surrounding the clearing, birds hopped through the sage and manzanita knowing they were protected by the burgeoning growth. Finches stopped singing and flew away. A pair of towhees that had been grubbing in the open scurried back into the undergrowth.

The coyotes paid no attention to the birdlife as they walked along the edge of the clearing toward the other side. They passed near a brush rabbit that sat frozen in an attempt to hide. The coyote's arrival caught the rabbit unaware and too far removed from the safety of the brush. The male coyote seemed not to notice, but with a sudden, quick, catlike pounce grabbed the rabbit about the head, shook it a few times and continued on, the rabbit dangling from its mouth.

Across the river below the level of the clearing, JR made his way upriver. He was walking along a narrow road several hundred feet above the river and below him the steep hillside was covered with white-flowering manzanita bushes that were preparing to set fruit, its little apples. The manzanita was interspersed with various oaks, some deciduous and some evergreen. Around him on the road, the earth became red. JR knew the road didn't go very far and that somewhere ahead there was a trail he could follow deep into the mountains. It'd been another year of drought, the snow level was high, and he had no idea how far he could go.

Growing up, JR had never really noticed the mountains. They held no interest for him. Though he had grown up at their feet, they'd been like a background noise – devoid of feature or detail – that slipped below his consciousness. One day though, he looked up midwinter to where the snow-covered peaks stretched across the horizon, suddenly full of a mystery he'd never perceived before, suddenly tilted and thrust up into his conscious mind like the vast tectonic plate beneath his feet that thrust upward to become the Sierra. The mysterious experience momentarily cut through the fog of his existence and set his destiny. JR felt as if he'd really seen them for the first time. The experience motivated him to retreat to the foothills and begin working the ranches after high school.

When JR's grandparents first moved to the area from Oklahoma right before World War II they lived in Linnell Camp, a ramshackle, flea-bitten labor camp down near Visalia and Farmersville, a short distance from the oak trees of the old swamp along the Kaweah River and all its creeks. JR's daddy, Tommy, was born in the camp and lived there until the family moved out to Tooleville at the foot of Rocky Hill. Both the places were now full of Mexicans living out the same kind of lives the Okies used to, but now with drugs and guns.

JR remembered going out to the cotton fields with his daddy one hot summer day during school vacation. His daddy was driving a big tractor and JR sat in the pickup as his daddy plowed up and down the endless rows of cotton, raising a cloud of dust. JR fiddled with the radio dial. The music was all Country and Western or Mexican. He caught the tail end of Johnny Cash singing about how he fell into a burning ring of fire, followed by Merle Haggard singing "Tulare Dust."

Tulare dust in a farmboy's nose,

It was all hardpan and dust, just hardpan and choking dust on the valley floor.

JR's life had seemed like hell and he hated the

fields of Tulare dust. The dust clogged his nose and his mind and the moment made it pretty clear. When he later looked up and noticed the mountains, he realized he could rise above the world he'd previously known. Riding horses through the foothills, no matter how hard the work, was far freer than life on the flatland, and there were certainly fewer people to deal with. He had a better relationship with his horse than any human he could think of, and for a while he lived his new freedom with abandon and happiness.

Now that he was finally walking on the road into the mountains he began to question his decision, the finality of it all. He was going to succeed in getting to the bottom of his pain or he was going to die trying. He envisioned walking toward the snow-choked backcountry and losing himself in the purity of the white snowfields, maybe swept into oblivion by an avalanche beneath some steep chute. No matter what occurred, things would be different, altered in some substantial way.

He thought of himself as bicultural, like a mixed-race person. His mother came from a family that moved to the San Joaquin Valley in the 1890s. When his parents married, his mother's parents viewed the whole thing with consternation. His mother's plans to complete college were put on hold when she met his father, and since education held no great truck with his daddy's family, she'd never returned.

When his mother's relatives came to visit, JR could see in their eyes that it was like they were visiting a third world country. The women were clucking and solicitous, and brought food and used clothing with them. Their kids tiptoed gingerly through the unkempt yards, wary of piles of accumulated dog shit, while any man that came along had little to say as he surveyed the junked cars in the yard.

Overhead a red-tailed hawk circled on a thermal. It spied the brush rabbit emerge from its cover, but a male coyote moved in too quickly. Across the river the red-tail could see the single human hiker moving along a road. The figure was gaunt and red, and even at the great distance the hawk's sharp eyes discerned other signs of fear and desperation. On the coyote's side of the river the hawk observed the two old men sitting by the river talking. The men were familiar sights to the red-tail. The hawk had seen them around the countryside since it first fledged. The men posed no threat. They seemed as substantial as the rock, though they seemed to move through the landscape like wind or water.

ALOFT
February 2009

The old men looked up toward the circling red-tail emitting its loud "scree." They were aware of the bird watching them for a few minutes before it turned its focus to something on the other side of the river. Either of the men could have reached out for an instant and shared the bird of prey's field of view, but for the moment they saw no need. There was no threat and they felt no curiosity. It was not yet time.

The men fell back into the time-shift of their memories. The past joined the present as time folded on itself.

When Wu first entered the Kaweah village along the river beneath the mountain peaks, he knew for certain he was in a different world. He was surprised when an old man at the edge of the village noticed him and approached in greeting. Later Wu learned the old man was named Yahpahkit. Yahpahkit led him to Francisco, who seemed to have been waiting for Wu's arrival. After their first meeting Wu and Francisco struggled to communicate with each other in their differing versions of English.

Though Francisco had been waiting for Wu for years, Francisco didn't expect someone from far across the ocean to the west. He'd seen, even boarded, the galleons of the Spanish in his days at San Luis Obispo, but there were no signs of any other people from the sea, other than a few Americanos. Since his datura-tahni vision of the Great Shark and the Grizzly Bear he'd had several dreams showing someone coming from the west, the direction in which the dead departed. He'd always assumed that the someone would be another Yokuts, maybe a Chumash, but not someone from where the sun set across the ocean. He was astounded by the idea of an ocean so vast that it took many months to sail across it in the big wooden ships. Over the years, Francisco had begun to doubt the power of the spirit world with all that had befallen his people, but the fact that this man could thread himself across the years and the great ocean to arrive at the village on the river was nothing short of a miracle. Wu's strange appearance, unlike either a white man or an Indian, made him seem like someone straight from a dream or vision.

Wu had no idea he was to meet someone. He was only aware of his quest to find a new home and of Dizang's admonition to find the truth expressed in a new way. The jagged range of peaks had seared itself on his mind and now he needed to find the exact place to carry on with his work.

Francisco broke free from the memory-shift and decided to allow his mind to be carried aloft by the red-tail circling above them. Below him spread the drainage of the Kaweah River as it plunged from the high peaks of the backcountry. While the hawk turned leisurely spirals in the uplift from the canyon walls, the old familiar landmarks circled before Francisco's vision. He remembered their old names from his own language, but he hadn't heard those names spoken in so many years that he ached at the memory of their sound in his mind. Nearby was an old Potwisha encampment at *Pahdin*, Hospital Rock, and along the road below Pahdin he could see a lone hiker. The Potwisha weren't Yokuts at all, but instead were a tribe of Mono who came from the other side of the mountains, though many times they inter-married. Pahdin meant "place to go under." Not only did the name refer to the cavern beneath the giant boulders where ceremonies were held, but it also referred to the fact the area was tripne, super-natural, a place to go beneath the world of appar-ent things and speak with the spirits. The rock had a large red painting meant to declare the supernat-ural quality of the boulder and the cave, but now it was just a curiosity for the tourists, located as it was across the road from a parking lot and picnic tables. Few people paused to look very closely and under-stand the old meanings.

When the hawk turned toward the mountains, a granite dome protruding thousands of feet above the river canyon came into view. The sides of the dome were peeling and falling away like the layers of an onion. Water that seeped into tiny cracks in the rock would freeze in winter and the expanding ice would create such force that layers of granite would be sloughed off the dome like old dead skin. The Americans called the dome Moro Rock and had built steps to the top of it. He had called it *Wahah Yahkow*, or High Rock, and sometimes during the summer the old men had travelled to the area when they followed game to the higher country or when they went to visit Old Man Tharp. Across the canyon from Wahah Yahkow stood the granite spires of Castle Rock, a place he called *Lungnotim*, the Undertakers. They seemed like guardians to the underworld where Tihpiknits the bird god dwelled. Up canyon between the two rock formations, the backcountry peaks loomed into his vision.

The jagged peaks were covered with snow and the sun in the western sky reflected off the white surface in a dazzling glare. He knew when the sun set tonight that its last dying light would flash in shades of rose off the icy faces of the granite peaks and mark the place where the sun would rise in the morning.

The hawk turned south and the jagged form

of Sawtooth Peak, *Kahdidit*, above Mineral King Valley, came into view. Francisco and Wu lived in a small cabin hidden off the winding road to the remote valley. To the west stretched the San Joaquin Valley lost in a haze. Most of the time the air was a hazy, polluted yellow-gray.

As he soared, the words came back.

My words are tied in one
with these great mountains,
With the great rocks,
with the great trees,
In one with my body
and my heart.
Do you all help me
with supernatural power,
And you, day,
and you, night!
All of you see me
one with this world!

Below him he observed the hiker.

Francisco shifted his mind again and was back along the river. Wu looked over inquiringly.

"Where'd you go this time? Up there?" Wu asked, as he nodded toward the sky.

The old men fell back in time again.

Francisco and Wu gradually got to know each other over the course of the following months. The green of spring gave way to the blast furnace of heat that was summer. Wu was acquainted with the hot humid air of southern China, but this heat was far different. It was bone dry. There were no summer rains to momentarily break the spell of the heat and the grasses dried yellow beneath his feet. Wu learned to constantly be aware for trah-ud, the rattlesnake, as he walked through the grass and over the rocks.

The river was a welcome respite with the trees along its banks – the sycamores, the cottonwoods, and the willows. He was given a hut in which to live in the village, but in the summer heat he slept many nights outside by the river. He rose early in the mornings and entered the water to perform his ablutions. Something in the lulling flow of the water worked its way through him and possessed him. It was indeed a strange new world.

Wu studied the people of the village. Many were dying and he did what he could to help. He struggled to learn the plant life of the area and understand its properties from Yahpahkit. It seemed the more he learned, the more the plants twined through him. He asked as many questions as he could, learned as much as he could, but the herbs had no great effect on the illness that gripped the people. The villagers succumbed quickly in ways that Wu had never before witnessed, though he seemed immune and unharmed.

During the time he watched the village die around him, Wu continued his own basic rituals to deal with his grief and powerlessness. He still rose at dawn to meditate in the new light after bathing, and he meditated at night before sleep. During the day he tried to help as best he could, however he could. Because Dizang told him to find a new way, Wu questioned Francisco often about his spiritual world and beliefs, until Francisco finally offered Wu an entry into the Kaweah spirit world so he could understand for himself. It was not only a gesture to the bear's prophecy, but Francisco also knew it was important for the future.

Yahpahkit was old and frail, and though he knew it would be an effort, he offered to gather and prepare the tahni for Wu's journey. The ceremony was conducted without much fanfare in the dying village. Wu went through the six cycles in the sweat lodge and then the six days of fasting. Francisco was the only one left with the energy and determination to support Wu's quest. Wu drank the bitter liquid and fought to control his stomach.

Francisco led Wu downriver to a cave on the side of the mountain above the north side of the river. It was on the side of one of the woman's thigh hills where the river entered the great valley. Above the cave entrance and to the right was a series of paintings that declared the tripne sacredness of the cave. Francisco left Wu at the entrance. Wu made his way inside the cave inside and allowed his eyes began to adjust to the dim light. Around him on the cave walls and ceiling emerged paintings of spirals and animal figures as well as human figures with split heads. In a far corner he made out the coiled sleeping form of trah-ud the rattlesnake trying to avoid the heat of the coming day. She'd been out hunting in the cool of the night. Wu felt fear at the snake's presence, but he was also determined to understand the spiritual world of Francisco and the Kaweah. He'd been sent here on a quest.

Wu moved further back into the cave until he found a place to lie down beneath an overhanging rock. Paintings covered the rock above his head and body and immediately before his eyes a spiral seemed to spring from the stone toward his mind. The spiral pulled him in as the tahni began to take effect.

The tahni moved through Wu's system and barriers between the worlds began to drop as the Great Mind made its presence more apparent. The spiral in front of his eyes swirled and carried him into an ancient memory. He was bowing in a great court surrounded by a group of men. They were scholars – holy men and learned men – and they were presenting themselves to the First Emperor. When his face touched the floor the scene shifted and he found he was buried in the ground up to his neck. Within his field of vision he could see the heads of the other scholars and holy men also protruding from the ground. The ground began to vibrate and shake as a herd of horses thundered into view driven by the emperor's guards. Clouds of dust rose in billows and the heads began to scream as the hooves collided with flesh and bone. Above him loomed a horse and a falling hoof. He muttered a prayer.

The prayer carried him to the river. He was floating in liquid, a fetus in a womb floating above the Kaweah where it passed between the woman's thigh portals in front of the cave. Wu felt a surge of fear when he realized he was going to be born once again. He dreaded being trapped in the helpless body of an infant for so long, unable to do anything more than thrash and cry. It was like being paralyzed or bound with ropes or buried helpless to his neck. His parents wouldn't understand his plight wouldn't know how to properly conduct him from one world into the other. They would simply bind him yet further with their beliefs and rituals, make him serve their needs and desires. The worst part would be being suffused in the thoughts and fears of the humans as they crowded around him. In past lives he'd had to forget his vast awareness and intelligence so he could endure the helplessness and fear. That was how he'd lived out the old lifetimes, forgetting so he could endure, then searching everywhere to regain what he'd lost. He didn't want to go through the cycles again.

It was different this time. The cave was now the womb and Wu was able to see his mother's face framed within his mind, the face of Guanyin, the goddess of mercy and compassion, the one who responds when suffering people cry out for help. Guanyin sensed his perception of her and smiled in his direction. Wu's fear ceased, his mind stilled and the suffering in the world around him no longer intruded.

Wu became a hungry infant and suckled at Guanyin's breast. While he nursed, a warm energy circulated throughout his body and he quickly grew in size. Soon he was too large for the cave and the mountain burst apart around him. He was thirsty for water, so he bent and swallowed the river. He was hungry for real sustenance, so he began to swallow the mountains – first the foothills around him and then the distant snowcapped peaks – yet when he finished they still remained unscathed. Wu then swallowed the whole of the earth, yet it remained. He turned to examine the emptiness between the stars. He swallowed the stars, but their light was undiminished, in fact there was even more light.

He took it all in. When he finished he was full. He knew the ten-thousand things and the vast empty space between the ten-thousand things, as well as the source of the ten-thousand things, and was full.

Wu stood before Guanyin. He was an old man, yet he still felt the circulation of energy from Guanyin's breast. Guanyin smiled. She wasn't dressed as a goddess or as anyone special. She looked more like one of the women of the tribe, one of the women on the verge of dying. Guanyin embraced him, kissed him on the forehead, and was gone.

Wu slowly regained his senses and focused again on the spiral over his head. It spun in reverse and pushed him back into the world. He looked slowly around the cave and noticed that trah-ud was now coiled next to his leg as if to protect him from any threat. Wu thanked her and began to carefully slide away, then paused for a second and touched the snake to bless it, all fear gone. He made his way to the mouth of the cave.

Wu followed the trail upstream toward the village and Francisco came to meet him. Old Yahpahkit had died. Back in the village Wu discovered that the disease and the suffering had ceased.

Wu moved back into the present, his back against a grey granite boulder and his eyes focusing upriver.

Francisco stood up and moved toward his friend. They looked out over the river below them. Here the river slowed down and formed deep pools just before the gorge narrowed and the river funneled through in a mass of whitewater. They stood for a few moments until Francisco heard a sound from the brush behind him. He turned to see a brown coyote emerge from among the dark red branches of the manzanita with a rabbit draped from its mouth. The female stayed back in the chaparral, barely visible. The coyote dropped the rabbit at the feet of the two men. Wu bowed his head slightly in the coyote's direction, then gestured with his open palm toward the rabbit.

"Thank you, but take it for yourself. She'll need it."

The coyote hesitated for a moment, then picked up the rabbit and disappeared back into the manzanita and buckbrush along with its mate.

BUCKEYE FLAT
February 2009

JR followed the road down a steep pitch toward the river where it ended at a park service campground that was closed for the season. The campground was named Buckeye Flat because it was set in a small forest of the skeletal white trees. The campground was at the bottom of the canyon, and the low winter sun on the southern horizon had not yet stimulated much new leaf growth. Only the tips of the topmost branches carried a smattering of green. Some of the trees still hung on to their giant seeds from the previous season, while at his feet some of the fallen seeds were beginning to split and sprout where there was enough warmth. The seeds were poisonous, and JR knew the Indians had ground them into a powder they threw into the river to stun fish.

JR walked on through the campground to the evergreen trees on the far side. He wanted to attract as little attention as possible, so he chose a place to camp back among the trees hidden from casual eyes. He rolled out his sleeping bag as he wondered how cold the night might get. Probably close to freezing. His sleeping bag was okay and he was hardy enough.

After all, he was a survivor of military training, surviving everything from desert heat to bitter nighttime cold. He'd also survived, as best he could, the worst that life could throw at him. With that thought he began to take a few things from his pack. He didn't have the initiative to cook and dark would be coming on soon. He broke out a few things to eat – some cheese, some bread.

The chill began to set in and JR lit a small fire. He stacked a few small dry twigs in a tepee shape over a crumpled food receipt he found in his pocket, then struck a match and carefully lit the paper. The fire sputtered, caught, and grew as he added more twigs and small branches.

JR reached into his pack and wrapped his hand around a small bottle of whiskey, leaned back against a tree, and took a sip. He was beginning to remember too much again. He'd hoped that heading into the mountains and being with the river would be an instant curative, that going into the old vision he had of the mountains would make the thoughts and memories go away, but the night was bringing back the memories along with the fear.

JR felt afflicted with what he called "wrongness" and he could never remember a time, except for rare instances, when he didn't feel the effects of the disease. The symptoms first developed when he was a child trying vainly to get his father's attention. JR could only attribute his isolation and lack of contact to being unacceptable – unacceptable and wrong. His sense of wrongness extended through his contacts with his mother's solicitous relatives, through his outcast school days, and into the military. His church even told him he was born a sinner. Though JR's days in Iraq were an attempt to do the right thing and make peace with his father's memory, he was constantly overwhelmed by the sense of being an unwanted presence. The stress and his constant witness to sudden death left him wrung out.

The level of everyday uncertainty was so high that he was always on edge and hardly slept. One day rolled into another in a hypnotic haze. He would close his eyes but nothing would go away. The war and the danger rolled through his fitful sleep until it seemed everything was a continuous unrelenting tidal wave of fear, uncertainty, and death. He'd walked into bombed out rooms where pieces of human beings were stuck to walls like chewing gum and even now the smell of seared human flesh sometimes came back to him and overwhelmed his ability to cope with the world. In his haze he fired blindly in the direction of gunfire and then sorted through the bodies – young and old, men and women – not knowing whether they were the enemy or not.

JR didn't know when life lost all meaning, when the mask was ripped off all his beliefs and any sense of hope. Growing up, he always held out hope for meaning, that if he had enough money, a house, a family, that life would snap into focus and become clear. Iraq had ripped it all away. How could he support any sense of normalcy or meaning on the back of what he'd seen and done?

When he was growing up it seemed there was a hole in his being through which demons could squeeze. He found if he struggled enough, got angry enough, he could keep fighting them back, but he had to be eternally vigilant. In Iraq the hole had been blown even larger by the first bomb, the one where the truck had been blown out from under him, three of his buddies killed, and him waking covered with their blood and pieces of their flesh. The bomb had blown a hole in his being big enough for a Humvee, or a tank, or a platoon to pass through, and through the hole had come a flooding throng of demons. It seemed like all the demons of all humanity. He continually struggled to plug the hole and to push the demons back to their source. Sometimes he slowed them, but he could never stop them. The winds blew through the hole in his mind and he didn't know where they came from or where they went. When he returned from the war, he looked for comfort again out in the mountains on his horse, attempted to pray, and drank.

He found Maria and slowed the demons, but she hadn't been able to comprehend the hole in his being, the longing, and the emptiness, let alone do anything about it.

He always returned to horses and these mountains. There was nothing else. The cowboy life was real, but now it wasn't working. He was hollowed out again, a bombed out ruin with wads of basic human hopes and dreams stuck to the walls, and there was a hand on his back pushing him toward an edge.

JR leaned back against a buckeye and took a drink of whiskey. For a golden moment the pain receded and the voices echoing from the emptiness fell silent. With it, the vision of making it deeper into the mountains began to disappear from his mind. Maybe he didn't need to look for the cold comfort of a high, icy pass – maybe the river was far enough. He doubted there could be anything more than this in life anyhow. Nothing in his own life indicated there was or could be. Though a part of him wanted to believe there was more, he didn't have enough energy left to sustain the foolish hope.

JR decided to walk upriver toward the bridge across the Kaweah to Paradise Falls. He wanted to recapture a memory of being there with Maria and feel her presence for a moment like he had in the cafe. He made his way unsteadily on the trail along the river. A full moon was shining overhead, and its light reflected in the flowing movement of the water. He stood for a moment on a sandspit covered with small water-smoothed granite rocks and studied the current as best he could.

When he came to the bridge he walked out half-way and looked up and down the canyon. Upriver toward Moro Rock the clouds descended from the mountains, the moon illuminating the face of the clouds and casting shadows along the river canyon. He thought he could see the moon shadow of a large fish swimming through a pool below the bridge. Maria swam through his mind in the pools on Paradise Creek and he tried to hold on to the memory, tried to feel her body. The night was quiet and cold and enforced an icy stillness on JR's mind. The longing arose and then subsided into impossibility.

JR moved to the railing and peered deeply into the dark water, startled at its beckoning familiarity. Without warning the earth heaved. The bridge began to buck in a sinuous rolling motion as if there had been an eruption among the dormant cinder cones in the backcountry or a temblor had rolled through from the bed of the ancient sea that formed the valley floor. JR fought to hold on to the rail, but was hurled from the bridge and into the black snowmelt cold of the river. As he flew through the air he thought he saw a light on the far side of the bridge in the direction of the falls and a dark bearded face. When he hit the water the current caught his body and carried him headlong into a boulder. His body tumbled in the whitewater and so did the world. Overhead, he caught twirling glimpses of the distant cold and uncaring stars, but lost them as he plunged beneath the surface again and again. The empty vacuum of space surrounded him and sucked at his mind, then the water pulled him down into the depths. He was beyond caring or struggling and welcomed the finality.

Downstream a large black shape ambled into the river.

ESHOM VALLEY
Spring 1870

Wu and Francisco surveyed the meadow in the middle of Eshom Valley. They were surrounded by thousands of Indians, both Yokuts and Mono, who'd made their way from the southern Sierra and the valley below. Some arrived on horseback, but most made the arduous trip on foot. Everyone was gathered at the meadow for the Heut Hetwe, the great new ghost dance to restore the land and bring back the dead from Tihpiknits Pahn.

The meadow was ringed by pine trees and the ground covered with sweet clover in bloom. Nearby a creek flowed by on its way to join what the settlers called Lime Kiln Creek, later Dry Creek, and behind them Shadequarter Mountain rose above Eshom Valley blocking the view of the snow covered mountains. The Yokuts called the place Chetutu, or Clover Place, and they were holding the dance of restoration here where there was water for drinking and bathing and fresh clover to eat.

Wu was transfixed by the sight of so many native peoples gathered in one place. He'd only dealt with small clusters of broken people scattered throughout the landscape during the ten years he and Francisco had been traveling in the mountains. After his tahni vision experience, the death of Yahpahkit seemed to dissolve the final glue that held the tribe together and the few remaining villagers moved away in different directions. Not only had Yahpahkit been Francisco's adviser and guide, he'd been the holder of the stories and ways for the tribe. Some of the tribe's members joined the Wukchumne across the river, some moved farther up into the mountains to join the remaining Potwisha at Hospital Rock, and some went to work at nearby ranches as vaqueros and cooks. They did what they could to avoid being sent to the reservation on the Tule River, which was jammed with many different tribes, both Yokuts and Mono. Over the years the Yokuts had become adept horsemen, seeming at one with the animals, and many ranchers valued their vaquero skills.

Francisco and Wu had moved into the mountains toward Hospital Rock and begun to roam the mountains. At times they supported themselves by working on ranches and on pack trains, Francisco putting his mission-learned vaquero skills to use, and Wu working as a cook.

The men heard the stories circulating through the mountains and out onto the plains about the Ghost Dance. The people were still dying from the

American diseases and several shamans from the Mono on the other side of the Sierra came to bring a new vision. If the people gathered and danced in a great circle for six days the suffering would cease, and the host of loved ones who'd died and now dwelled in Tihpiknits Pahn would return. The land would also be returned, returned to them restored in its abundance and meaning.

Shamans with hats of tall hawk feathers that pointed toward the sky began to direct the dance. The people, filled with earnest sacred hope, began a slow sideways shuffle. Designated paid singers, the Ahanich, sang their plea to the spirits, while at times the shuffling dancers joined with the words.

I will be anything
Hah-nah nahn een-ah nah-ne
Hah-nah nahn een-ah nah-ne
Hah-nah nahn een-ah nah-ne
Hah-nah nahn een-ah a-a

I will be anything –
crow, rock, stick,
rattlesnake or anything –
if our ones who are dead
could come back
to us, in this world.

Francisco and Wu noticed settlers intersperse themselves throughout the crowded meadow trying to track everything going on, suspicious the Indians planned an attack. Occasionally the settlers half-heartedly joined in the dancing as if to disavow their presence, despite their pale skins and bristling beards.

Across the meadow a settler stood by a wagon loaded with small barrels and called out drunkenly.

"Whiskey, I got whiskey!"

He held out a half-empty bottle toward anyone who passed. He envisioned making a small fortune from the horde of hopeless, drifting souls. The dancers ignored him, and focused on their sacred quest. For the moment they had hope and they had direction. Restoration and peace were far more important than whiskey, a return of fathers and mothers, brothers and sisters more important than a momentary blind drunk. They had a chance to touch the Great Spirit and know their purpose.

At times, Wu was nearly overcome by the fierce mix of hope and sorrow. Other times he joined with Francisco in the dancing, both to understand the Indians and to be part of them. As he danced the rip currents of desperation that lurked beneath the surface of the dance tore at him. His sense of compassion, his Buddha's compassion, had been like a cool, distant observation of life, but being thrown into the circling, churning dance overwhelmed his careful distance. He wanted to heal things, wanted to relieve the massive suffering, but felt overwhelmed at the magnitude of the pain. The people were dancing to be released from the hell created for them on earth through no fault of their own. Dizang was supposed to be able to emancipate, to free, the souls of those in hell. Dizang was in Wu and yet Wu felt powerless in the face of so much raw suffering. The dance altered him and altered his very sense of compassion.

Francisco watched as his people danced this strange new Ghost Dance, one that had never been part of his experience, of any Yokut's experience. Though it seemed there were a great many people at the dance, Francisco knew that only one person in ten had survived since the time he came back from the mission. The knowledge and ways were mostly gone and his people were clinging to the visions of a man from across the mountains. Francisco prayed with all his heart for the restoration of the world and his people to happen, but he didn't hold out much hope that it would happen. How could a dance overcome the guns, fear, prejudice, and greed aligned against the Yokuts? It was good to see all the people together, even if dancing a foreign dance, but Francisco feared there was a price to pay for blind, vain hope. He would trust the vision more if it sprang from the very ground on which they walked on this side of the mountains.

Francisco and Wu watched the dancers circle night and day, broken by calls from the chiefs to go to the creek and bathe for purification. By the end of the fifth day, a deep, dusty rut was worn into the ground – the clover beaten down to nothingness – and the pool of the creek was only a muddy hole. That night, before the dance could be completed, a rumor began circulating that settlers were coming with guns. In fear and panic, the dancers and seekers scattered in the dark and hid wherever they could in the folds of the mountains. Francisco and Wu headed around Shadequarter Mountain and down to the North Fork to follow the river back to the main fork of the Kaweah.

That which was gone had not returned.

Despair weighed heavily on Francisco after the Ghost Dance. He hadn't expected any success, but the dashed hope of his people tore at his spirit. He heard they tried to do the dance again down near Farmersville for the whole six days, but like before, nothing was returned or restored. The Americans themselves could have planned no better way to break what remained of his people's spirit – building a false final hope then dashing it with abject failure. It was certainly a trickster's bargain. Despite the power of his connection to the world of the spirits, he was unable to bring the spirit power to the everyday world in such a way as to alter the course of his people's suffering.

Unfortunately the bear had been right about his people's fate. The only things that kept him going – and stabilized in the face of this devastation of spirit – were his friendship with Wu and the power of the bear in his middle. When despair attacked Francisco, Wu and the bear stood with him to keep the darkness at bay. Between them, they became a great rock that the floodwaters swirled around, but couldn't move.

Sometimes Francisco spread himself on the ground and sometimes he immersed himself in the river so he could release the pain he felt into the earth or into the swirling, moving water. Without the embrace of this landscape and his friend, without the flow of energy from the ground up through the soles of his feet he couldn't survive, nor would he want to. He loved the beauty of this world. He didn't understand how anyone could work so hard, so joylessly, to bring such suffering and destruction to the realm of the living. He had done what he could. Maybe he was simply too impure to end this unnecessary suffering.

John Woods' bloody face swam into Francisco's mind. Francisco once more regretted what he'd done and prayed to the spirits. What was done was done. There was nothing more he could do.

BELOW PARADISE
February 2009

JR's body surged and plunged through the water while the stars tumbled and rolled through his mind. The current accelerated into whitewater and carried him headfirst into another rock. He gasped and fought to keep the water from filling his lungs. The water pulled him under for what he thought would be the last time when he caught a glimpse of a large dark body and felt his shoulder crash into something solid and immovable that wasn't rock. Just as his mind collapsed into unconsciousness, he thought he felt wet matted fur followed by the sensation of being pulled with great power from the river.

The old men who waited for JR had paid a great price for their longevity. Most every person that Francisco and Wu had known over the years was gone – dead, buried, and moldered in the ground. The landscape had changed – forests cut down, rivers dammed, rolling hills leveled, the delta covered by streets and houses. Their memories of all the losses witnessed over the years was a devastating blow if they dwelled on them. The old men laughed at the notion of how immortality might seem a lucrative offer. They knew most people would actually be crushed by the collective weight of memory, history, knowledge, and powerlessness. There was also the loneliness, always the human loneliness. They had each other, but humans were meant to dance in larger circles.

Something pulled the old men past the devastations and toward their purpose.

JR came to consciousness with the two old men hovered over him, the darker one pumping on his chest. He coughed up water and then felt his wet clammy clothes. The first light of dawn appeared upriver and a cold breeze blew down the canyon and over his body. He began to shake. One of the old men, the one who looked Asian, handed JR a blanket and helped JR to pull it around himself tightly. JR couldn't quite place the other old man. He could have been Mexican, but maybe he was an Indian. JR looked down at his body and examined his scrapes and abrasions. It seemed he was lucky he still had skin. Several places on his body had long scratches as if some large animal had raked at him.

The old men told him their names. Wu and Francisco. Francisco lit a fire behind a boulder as JR moved next to the flames for warmth. The old men didn't say much. They just sat and watched him as the fire warmed him and he stopped shivering.

JR didn't know what to say. He simply mumbled a thank you and stared at the ground. When the sun rose above the peaks and began to flood the upper walls of the canyon with light, the old men put out the fire and gestured at JR to get up. JR was usually a contrarian when it came to anyone telling him what to do, but for the moment he simply followed the old men's lead.

The old man called Wu grabbed a walking stick made of manzanita and began to lead an upstream scrambling trek through brush and across rocks toward the Paradise Creek bridge. The old men moved quickly as they carried nothing more than a little food and a couple of blankets. When they came to the bridge, JR looked at it closely. After his experience of the previous night, he fully expected the bridge to be gone, or at least severely damaged from the jolt, but it appeared the same as ever.

They walked together to the campground where the old men quickly gathered JR's pack and other belongings as if they already knew where they were. When they began to ascend the road, the light struck the foliage around them and warmed the flowers and leaves. The smell was fresh and pungent and circulated through JR's head until he could taste the landscape around him. For a moment he was awake.

When they arrived at the parking lot JR saw his truck still parked where he'd left it. A few spaces away, JR saw an old GMC truck from the fifties. Francisco pushed JR into the passenger side of JR's truck then took the wheel. Wu climbed into the old men's truck, started it with several cranks of the starter, then pulled out onto the highway and headed down the mountain. Francisco followed with JR. Despite the chaos and strange events of the night and morning, JR fell asleep and began to dream while Francisco negotiated the turns down the mountain.

The landscape around him was white with snow and ice and his body was cold. He could scarcely feel a thing, but he had to keep moving, just keep moving, and if he stopped he'd die. He sensed he was being stalked and tried to watch in all directions at once, but the hyper-vigilance was becoming as exhausting as the cold. Every step could be the wrong step and no step at all would bring an icy death. He couldn't remember how he got there or why he was there. The only thing he could remember was the seeming interminability of his journey through time and the constant knife-edge of the cold piercing him through and through.

He looked around for signs of habitation and warmth, but found none. The gray-skied open plain he'd been traversing changed into dense forest and the gathering trees added a black looming mass of darkness to the cold. Behind every tree was a shadow and a fear. He heard a huffing and puffing behind him and turned to find a grizzly bear plodding toward him through the snow and ice, its hot breath forming a cloud in the cold air. He tried to outrun it, but couldn't. The bear grabbed him and dragged him to the edge of a hole in the snow-white world and then jumped with him into the void.

JR woke up and looked around. He was seated on the passenger side of his truck with no one else around. The truck was parked next to the old GMC, which in turn was parked next to a small cabin nestled under oak trees and a few pines. On the other side of the cabin was a small stream. He turned and realized he was on a mountainside above a canyon where a river plunged down the mountain and formed waterfalls and rapids that caught the morning light. The larger trees along the creek behind the cabin gave way to manzanita and scrub oak vegetation that carried down to the granite walls above the river. He guessed he was somewhere above the East Fork of the Kaweah, somewhere on the way up to Mineral King, but he couldn't tell exactly where.

Wu approached the truck and rapped on the window with the head of his walking staff. The sound shot through JR's mind, still addled from alcohol, water ingestion, and a groggy recovery from the dream world. Wu gestured for him to get out of the truck and go into the cabin. JR walked through the doorway and looked around at the simple, but well-kept furnishings. An old wood-fired stove dominated a cooking area. JR assumed it was also used to heat the place. Next to the stove, a few counters and shelves lined the wall. There was also a small wooden table with several wooden chairs. Strangely, a single electric bulb hung above the table, though JR hadn't seen any power lines and doubted these old men would have a generator. At the other end of the room was a small couch along with a few more chairs, and next to the couch was a bookcase full of books.

Wu leaned his staff in a corner and motioned for JR to sit at the table. Sometime after he experienced the immensity of suffering at the Ghost Dance, Wu felt compelled to begin carrying a staff. Dizang always carried a staff, a staff with six rings dangling from the top. Monks carried similar staffs and shook the jangling rings as they walked, a signal to wild animals. No surprises, no attacks. Wu had no need for the rings – the animals gave the old men passage wherever they went anyway. Even the rodents and insects allowed them this cabin as a haven with no intrusion.

Dizang's six rings represented the six worlds he vowed to save, but Wu knew only this world.

This world was it, the fulcrum. Wu chose to make his staff from a branch of manzanita, dark red with streaks of weathered grey. At the upper end was a small burl that he carved into a likeness of Dizang's head. Dizang carried his staff to batter on the gates of Hell and force them open if he could. He vowed that he would not be free until all beings were free. Wu had no such grandiose thoughts for himself. There was scarcely a person on the planet who knew of his existence. All he could do was walk through his life, aided by the manzanita staff, and teach the few he could – maybe help free them.

Wu prepared tea and brought it to the table just as Francisco walked into the room. Hot green tea had never been on JR's list of preferred drinks. His life had been more about diner or campfire coffee – maybe big glasses of sweet ice tea at barbecues. It wasn't that he hated the drink. It was just alien to him and seemed weak and unmanly. Maria had been into different kinds of tea, but he always resisted the offers because the drink couldn't provide the jolt that he needed to face the day and his life.

Wu poured three cups of tea then sat down at the table while Francisco watched from a chair in the living area. Wu sipped his tea and studied JR silently for what seemed an eternity. In the long silence, JR struggled to find words for his questions, but the absence of sound was a dead weight on his mind.

There had been long silences with Maria when he had no words to describe what was going on for him. It felt like there was a transparent wall with a door between them, and he didn't even know how to reach out and turn the knob. As he turned inward thinking about the silence and the knot in his guts, he didn't notice Wu get up and retrieve the stick from the corner. When JR finally looked up, Wu raised the handle in front of his face. He caught a glimpse of a carved head at the top of the stick just at the moment Wu brought it down and tapped him emphatically three times on the forehead. At the third tap, JR imploded inward toward the knot at the center of his being and fell to the floor weeping. The knot exploded, snot rolled from his nose, and he shit in his pants.

The old men covered him with a blanket, then each of them touched JR's belly with their palms. They picked up their cups of tea and walked out into the day to watch the river far below.

JR lay on the floor in a semi-conscious state, his mind swirling in a vortex. In the vortex he made out faces and forms and feelings. He saw his father, tormenting Okie classmates, and dead friends from Iraq with half-missing faces. There were also faces of dead Iraqis looking at him, bloodied and accusing. He felt fear and anger and betrayal and he could smell death, urine, and shit. Beyond the identifiable faces rolled wave upon wave of chaotic, unknown visages that seemed to extend back through indeterminate time.

The place in his belly, where the knot had been, began to expand outward and as it did, it formed a bubble that began to push all the faces and forms and feelings away from his mind. The bubble extended away from his body a short distance in all directions until the totality of things that assaulted him stood outside the bubble and outside his body. JR watched the faces and forms and feelings swirl outside the shield and he began to feel still, even though the storm continued to rage.

After an hour, Francisco and Wu came back into the room. They helped JR to his feet and escorted him outside where they helped him out of his clothes. Wu grabbed some rags along with a pail of water that had been standing in the sun and the two old men helped JR bathe himself. After JR was clean he sat down on a nearby stump to regain his equilibrium, but before he could settle for too long, the old men each took one of his elbows and guided him down to the creek where it fell into several pools. Francisco and Wu moved JR toward a pool that was bathed in afternoon sunlight and had him sit down in the swirling flow of water. When he sat he began to slightly float in repose as the water swept along his skin. He watched occasional leaves drift by in the current. JR was still surrounded by the bubble field and he felt the water carry the dark forms and feelings away in its flow and convey them down the mountain toward the East Fork.

JR had no idea how long he floated in the water in the patch of light. He didn't even notice the cold – in fact he seemed to generate heat internally. When the shadows began to creep toward him, the old men returned and helped him back to the house where they handed him his pack with clean clothes. They showed him a place in the room where he could roll out his sleeping bag. Though he hadn't eaten all day, he felt no hunger as he fell into a deep and dreamless sleep.

JR awoke with the dawn and slowly got up and looked around, but found no sign of the old men. During the entire day's strange events, not one word had been spoken except for being told their names. When JR searched his memories and tried to understand what had happened, he found only confusion. It was as if he'd walked through a dreamscape the entire day, a hallucination populated with improbabilities and impossibilities. With a jolt, he remembered yesterday morning's dream of falling into the bottomless void in the grasp of the bear. Somehow he'd ended up in the cabin by the creek above the river. He looked around. It was real. But, he didn't know if his experience was.

JR poked around the cabin and found a note on the table. It instructed him to come back in two weeks. He packed his things, then climbed into his truck and pointed it downhill along the dirt and gravel road toward the river. He trusted it would lead him to a paved road that could take him home.

THE VORTEX
March 2009

In the years that cascaded like a river after the Ghost Dance, Francisco and Wu sat together in front of many fires. Across the flames and the smoke they'd discuss their situation and try to plumb the depths of their stories. The two old men came from different places on the planet and different cultures, yet they shared their common fate of endless years and an awareness that grew within the mystery of that ceaseless fate. They entertained each other with their stories of Coyote, Bear, and Prairie Falcon, and of the Buddha, Lao-Tsu, Guanyin, and Dizang.

"Dizang told me I had to cross the Eastern Ocean and come to these mountains where I found you," Wu said. "He said I was supposed to go beyond the Buddha and Lao-Tsu, but I still don't know what that means. Maybe I'll find out."

Wu looked at the ground almost apologetically. He still didn't know if his friend would understand.

"After he told me those things, he stepped inside me."

Francisco looked at Wu with amazement and laughed. "Grizzly Bear told me you'd come, then I became water and he dove inside me.

"It was like this."

Francisco moved away from the fire and dove into the river to show Wu the truth.

They told more and more stories to each other over the years until the old men dropped out of the bottom of the stories into a common vastness.

Occasionally Francisco and Wu returned to the area around Badger and Eshom Valley where the Ghost Dance had been held. It seemed as if the dance had created a Vortex of unfulfilled spiritual longing that engulfed the area, a longing for a world and way of life that was more real and fulfilling than the one that currently existed. Over the years the old men had seen spiritual groups come and go in the area in response to the empty echoes of the Ghost Dance. There had been Synanon and Balladullah, the City of Allah, whose ruined buildings stood as testimony to the inability to go beyond fear and desire. There were even Hare Krishnas and Subuds living in the midst of cowboy country. The Vortex relentlessly pulled at the mind and the old men found it was an exercise of personal will to hold themselves intact in the midst of this storm of unrelieved suffering and longing.

The Vortex had finally eroded JR's life in the mountains. He escaped the flatlands and the war in order to find some peace simply riding his horse in the mountains among the trees and rocks and rivers, beyond the need to deal with very many people, but he couldn't evade the circling suffering of the Ghost Dance. He wanted to be alone, yet couldn't be alone. He tried to run away from ghosts only to attract more.

Throughout his life, JR had felt the normal human desire to belong with others, but he also felt burned and destroyed by the relationships he'd had. He always held out the slim hope that somewhere he'd find someone to help him understand the mess that passed for his life – that passed for life in general.

He put the weight of all that on Maria, but she just up and left without a word nearly two years ago. He remembered how it was when they first met and first made love. They'd touched for quite awhile and then when he entered her it was like an entry to another world, a world where he dissolved and expanded without any sense of who he had been or was. Sliding and dissolving, sliding and dissolving. He was both frightened and entranced by the power of her vagina over him. While making love he could momentarily forget his torment and suffering, but he always had to return to himself far too quickly. When he laid back and surveyed her body – and the portal that existed between her legs – he could feel the pain begin to return and shrivel his being. He wanted to have a future with her, but didn't know how to communicate through the pain that filled the time between their moments of passion.

He'd never been allowed to voice a desire and have it come true and so found it difficult to have much of a voice at all. Maria had gotten all caught up in the new-age stuff about creating what you desire by thinking the right thoughts. When Maria told him he should imagine success or good things happening he laughed loudly and desperately in his mind. She didn't have a clue that he had no ability to imagine those things. He had no real basis in his life to even believe it possible. He had no basis for belief in anything other than failure.

Maria had simply left and he'd never pursued her despite how much he cared. Her leaving simply added to the weight of his failure. In response he simply disappeared into the hills as much as he could to care for the cattle, and when he wasn't there, he was drinking again. He figured she was just tired of him and his failures.

JR's experience with the old men subverted everything, subverted a whole lifetime of failed experience. When he returned home he spent the first day walking along the creek and up into the hills trying to make sense of everything. He'd only been gone a few days, but it seemed like he'd experienced his entire life in the flash of a moment.

After the first day back he tried to busy himself with the routine of work, but things were slow. The first few days seemed like living in a paradise. JR couldn't remember a time in his life when he felt so free of his pain. He wasn't really free though, it was more like the pain was at arm's length so it couldn't touch him. He still sensed something outside his skin that kept the demons at bay.

He also began to think of Maria again. The thought of her aroused him and brought on feelings of tenderness, the feelings laced with fear.

JR made a few phone calls to find out where she was living, and as he did so he felt the field around him begin to weaken and let in the hot breath of the lurking demons.

That night JR dreamed of her. She walked up to him in the middle of an oak forest and wore a long flowery dress that opened at the top to expose her breasts. JR felt both his mind and body become aroused, felt a current of energy tingling through his limbs. He wanted to embrace her and feel her breasts, to make love, but instead she extended her hand toward him. JR extended his own hand toward her and when he did so she dropped an acorn into his waiting palm. Several times he turned the acorn over to examine it, but when he looked up again she had disappeared. When he moved forward to look for her, he became engulfed in a dense gray fog. Vines hung from nearby trees and in the distance he heard the muffled sound of quarreling crows in the treetops. Close at hand he could hear the sound of a river.

In the morning JR decided to drive down to the flatland where Maria lived. He drove up to the Mountain House for breakfast again, then pointed his truck down Dry Creek Road toward the Valley. As he drove, he studied the scenery and tried to understand the dream from the night before. He still felt the longing and the arousal, but he had no clue what it meant and had no idea how Maria would react to seeing him.

JR passed the cowboy poet's ranch and reached the bottom of Dry Creek Road where the river spreads itself out through the trees and thickets like a bayou. When he drove on the bridge across the river he began to smell the faint wafting scent of orange blossoms. JR knew that within a week or two the area would be permeated with the sweet citrus smell and that farther down in the valley the peaches, plums, and almonds were beginning to blossom into seas of white, pink, and red.

JR followed the highway into the flatland where Maria lived. He knew it was somewhere along one of the branches of the river near Venice Hill and the old place they called Woodsville, though nothing remained. He drove through remnants of the old oak forest spread along the distributaries of the river and the oaks and the river rekindled the dream about Maria. He crossed several bridges then found the mailbox with her address. She lived in a small house set back in the walnut orchards of a larger ranch that was accessed by a long driveway back through the groves.

JR was fond of the walnut orchards, their stately canopies providing cool shade on hot summer days. The trees thrived on the sandy rich soils that accumulated over the years when the branches of the river once overflowed their banks. He was glad he wasn't around though, when harvest happened and the shaker trucks moved down the orchard rows grasping and violently shaking the trees until all the nuts fell. The air would become full of dusts and molds in billowing clouds that mingled with the yellow-gray smog of summer and fall.

JR approached Maria's small house and studied it for a moment. The house was an old white clapboard-sided farmhouse built on raised foundations with hydrangeas along the front. As he walked up to the front porch and to the door, the doubts and terrors started to gain a beachhead in his mind.

He knocked.

When the door opened, Maria stood in the opening, and JR realized he had no idea what to say. He wanted to turn around and leave, but just as he was about to, his eyes scanned the room behind Maria and noticed a small child, a toddler with light brown skin and bronze hair. He stood at the door for a few moments longer. Maria finally beckoned him in and gestured toward the sofa where they could sit and talk. JR settled into place and the child crawled up on the cushion between them.

At first the child looked away shyly, but after a few moments reached out and grasped JR's index finger.

CAUGHT IN THE RUSH
March 2009

JR could still remember when the rush of sexual energy first happened. He was twelve, and the glimpse of a breast and then a nipple as a girl classmate bent over caused him to feel a flush throughout his body. His pants began to bulge and he struggled between wanting to run away to hide and wanting to stay and somehow be able to reach out and touch the fruit. It was the first real feeling of pleasure he could remember in his life. He felt suddenly pulled out of his everyday fears and concerns and brought to one-pointed concentration on his arousal and its immediate cause. He began to dream of breasts and the unimaginable place between a girl's legs and soon after that glimpse he awakened from a dream feeling a hot rush from his erect and outsized penis. The quest to experience this pleasure with a girl became his reason for being alive. He imagined that the pleasure would somehow make up for the pain and fill the emptiness he felt.

He'd felt anxious all his life, constantly wary as he searched his landscape for the next threat, the next insult, or next impending failure. The anxiety was like an electrical current that seemed to propel him fitfully ahead as if he was tumbling down a hill or being carried through rapids. Now he could imagine some relief from the spasmed propulsion of anxiety. The two feelings became increasingly linked, so that whenever he felt anxiety, he could imagine its relief in the form of sexual arousal until eventually anxiety and arousal blurred together. His anxiety and fear began to bring on an arousal that insistently demanded some form of momentary satiation in order to end the anxiety. He was tossed in unending tumbling cycles.

At some point in the future he would ask Francisco how he'd been able to survive those cycles of whitewater turbulence in his life.

"You used your imagination."

"But all I thought of was sex and getting away."

"You used your imagination. It kept you going for one more day."

JR would come to understand that if he simply took away his desires and addictions with nothing to replace them, there would be a void to his daily life that he could never endure. He had to use his imagination for something else before he could let his desires go away. Even though his desires had never been fulfilled for longer than a moment, the attempt to fill them had propelled him forward.

Most of the women he'd had sex with were only anxiety-ending objects that he used to find a momentary cessation from pain. It had been difficult for him to stop and listen to whatever cares or concerns the women might have because it would only add to his own restless anxiety for which they were supposed to be the cure.

"What should I use my imagination for, then?"

"Redemption."

"What do you mean by that?"

"That's your task – to find out."

It had been different when he was out riding through the hills and mountains. The geographical shapes of the landscape combined with the colors and forms of the plant life had brought on a different type of arousal. Being in the mountains mostly kept his anxieties at bay, so what he felt was a deep desire to be part of all the color and form he perceived. The landscape touched him more deeply than any human ever had. It touched him in ways that he wished humans could, especially a woman. He wanted to make love to a woman and have her be the landscape, to not only be touched that deeply, but to be able to communicate his erotic, passionate, secret feelings back to the shapes and colors of the natural world.

At times it seemed as if the entire mountain range was a lover in repose.

The fact that he couldn't touch either a woman or the landscape in that way furthered his despair and the despair was an opening to the Vortex.

Maria came closer than any of the rest, but he still felt a barrier inside to the expression of this world of color and form. Even though he loved her as best he could, he couldn't say much about this other world. He didn't have any words. He wished somebody could give him the words or the means of expression.

The moment JR realized the child sitting next to him was his own, he felt like he'd been struck by Wu's stick again, but without the side effects. A multitude of feelings coursed through him and traced colors.

After contemplating what Francisco told him, JR's future self imagined reaching back to the man on the couch. Time folded and he imagined redemption.

JR had no idea how to go about being a father. It was all he could do to make it from day to day and the thought of the ongoing responsibility overwhelmed him. Part of him was angry that Maria had gotten pregnant and put him in this position. His child was a girl, and even through his anger he knew it was a good thing. Normally a man was supposed to desire a son to carry on the family name and the father's pride, but he knew if his child had been a boy, then every one of the boy's actions would have conjured scenes and feelings from JR's own past. He knew his anger could take over at times and he was afraid he'd get carried away and treat his own son the way he was treated by his own daddy. He'd avoided becoming trapped in parenthood because he knew he wasn't fit and he didn't want any child to have to endure what he'd endured.

It was clear why Maria had left. She knew he wasn't up to the task. The moment he looked closely at his daughter next to him, a feeling of love and tenderness made its way past the fear. When she smiled shyly at him he reached out to pick her up and place her on his lap.

He sat wordlessly with his daughter for nearly a half hour. He didn't feel the anger anymore, but he didn't know how to react to the situation either. All the erotic thoughts he'd conjured about seeing Maria again deserted him.

JR rose from the couch and handed the child to Maria, then stood in front of them, still fighting for words.

"Look, I don't know what to say about all this, but I'll talk to you soon as I figure something out. I'm not running away."

JR reached out and touched his daughter's face with love. Somehow the old men had made things different, but he had no idea where the difference was going to lead.

Maria looked at him and nodded as JR awkwardly leaned over and kissed her on the cheek.

"Her name is Sophia."

VISITORS
March 2009

The days were warmer and spring was coming, so the old men began to work in the garden next to their cabin. They dug and turned the soil, soil that had built up over the last hundred years, then turned their attention to inspecting and repairing the drip irrigation lines that were fed by the creek. A small solar collector stood in a clearing and powered a creekside pump in addition to powering the single light in their house. Every once in a while one of them would remember how they'd found the equipment and would begin to laugh. Sometimes they'd tell the story to each other at a fire, embellish the story each time, and laugh even more.

On one of their trips up the mountain they discovered a marijuana plantation that had just been raided, and on impulse took the irrigation equipment before it could be hauled away. Better to make use of it, they thought, as they gleefully carried it down to their cabin. They were always coming across illicit farms in the mountains but never did much about it except to play mischievous tricks on the workers and guards. Everybody was so serious about the whole damned thing and it was amusing to watch the perplexed reactions. Sometimes at night the growers would imagine they heard a massive animal moving through the plantings and in the morning they found enormous tracks. Other times things would simply be moved or go missing.

A few days after the old men returned with their booty, they came across one of the Mexican growers unconscious on the ground. He'd run away in a panic at the sound of the helicopter when the patch was raided, and wandered around the mountains, disoriented with no food. He'd been unable to find the creek again or any other water source in the summer heat. The old men took him in until he recovered. The man was tiny, even by Wu's standards, only five feet tall, and had long hair and a beard that made him look like Christ, though his body below his neck was a mass of tattoos. They began to call the man Jesusito, even when he protested and said it wasn't his name. Jesusito could never figure out why he'd never seen the cabin before.

Jesusito spoke only Spanish, but the old men both knew the language. Francisco learned in his mission days and Wu picked it up over the years as a matter of necessity. Jesusito stayed with them while he recuperated and helped the old men tend things around the cabin. Over the years other people had spent time at the place, mostly as charity on the old men's part. Down deep Francisco and Wu held the hope of finding someone curious and inquisitive enough to observe them, ask questions, and stick around, but no one had. It seemed something endemic to the area, this general lack of curiosity about things. It seemed like a curse on the landscape.

Sometimes when a guest was around, their proximity to the old men allowed the guests' dreams to be entangled with the dreams of the old men. Though all the dreams were about the same thing, they manifested in different forms. Wu might talk with Dizang or Guanyin, while Francisco entered the world of Tihpiknits or flew with Limik the prairie falcon. The guest meanwhile might dream of winning the lottery or screwing his favorite movie star, waking up with a hard-on and a desire that couldn't be fulfilled.

Jesusito was no different from those who preceded him. The dreams heightened his desires and his need to fulfill them, even if for only a moment. When people left the old men and the cabin, their memories of the place quickly degraded to a fine dust on their feet. All that remained were the random thrashings of their kindled desires. When Jesusito left he quickly met up with some of his friends from the weed farm and tried to take them back to the cabin while he still had a small memory of it. It was difficult to remember the way back, though, and even when he passed the cabin by chance, his eyes glanced past it as if his mind refused to acknowledge or comprehend the place. Once in awhile Francisco and Wu would see Jesusito down in Three Rivers, but his eyes never showed a glimpse of recognition.

Jesusito turned out to be a bit different from the other visitors. Some impulse continually drove him back to the area of the cabin. Francisco and Wu would find him at various times collapsed along a trail or road with various afflictions. It might be a sprained ankle or dehydration or sheer exhaustion. Once the old men even saved Jesusito from snakebite. Fortunately the rattlesnake was saving its venom for something it could actually eat, and though Jesusito was hysterical, he wasn't close to dying.

Each time the old men found him, Jesusito would cry out to them in Spanish, "Thank God, you have found me," as if he'd never seen them before in his life.

Francisco and Wu took Jesusito in and nursed him to health and every visit, Jesusito proudly showed off his tattoos, especially the newest one from his latest journey into the world. After a week or two Jesusito's desires would stir up again and he'd wander back to civilization. He'd forget everything, as usual, then find his old friends and get another tattoo to mark his cycles. Eventually he'd be drawn back to the vicinity of the cabin again. It became a running joke for the old men. At every bend in the trail or road they made bets as to whether they'd find Jesusito, waiting helpless by the trail.

"Senors. Thank God, you have found me. You have saved me."

The old men never took offense at the leavings or tried to compel anyone to stay. Francisco remembered what it was like to be shackled to the mission and the padres, shackled and beaten by people who were sure they knew what was best for his soul. Francisco and Wu always felt a loss when their guests fled. They were simply humans with a basic need for friendship and companionship no matter how long they'd lived. There was no way they could compel anyone to be curious, no way to compel anyone to desire their knowledge, so the old men had to accept their human loneliness as just the way it was. They couldn't fully push away the sorrow away or eliminate it, but neither could they allow themselves to wallow in it.

Francisco and Wu turned the soil and prepared it for new planting, then talked briefly about JR. He was due back soon, if he indeed chose to come back. It was the first time they'd devoted much of any energy to thoughts of him. They both treated JR's presence matter-of-factly, without much in the way of speculation. They didn't hope for a different outcome for this particular encounter, but knew it would be different because of the raven's message. Francisco was even surer in his conviction. They knew however, that even if signs and intuitions pointed in a certain direction, the outcome was never guaranteed. Trickster Coyote and random chance always had free rein in people's lives if they weren't aware.

Spring was coming on. Soon the hills would be covered with the flame of redbud trees in full bloom and the air electric with the humming of bees through all the wild blossoms. With the short snows of the preceding winter the mountains would begin to open up before long. The old men looked forward to going up to Mineral King and roaming through the backcountry again. Every time he returned, Wu was reminded of Dizang's admonition and of the peaks' magnetic presence.

When JR returned home from seeing Maria and meeting his daughter he felt overwhelmed at the onslaught of new information that he couldn't process. It wasn't just that he couldn't process it, there was simply no more room in his mind. In addition to his new experience, his mind was also inundated with memories and feelings of childhood and of his daddy. The memories of the stress and violence of war had also returned. Beyond that he felt impinged upon by things he didn't understand, by unnamable forces and fears that didn't even seem to emanate from him. Now he was being asked to make room in the midst of all that for not only Maria, but also a child. Everything that had transpired up at the cabin off Mineral King Road seemed a strange dream, and whatever clarity and peace JR had gained was gone.

JR was conflicted about returning to see the old men. In the first few days after returning home from their cabin it seemed as if his state of mind would be that way forever, and there would be no need to return. JR was loathe to be dependent on anyone, even after the profundity of his experience. People were never dependable and he didn't want to tether himself to that undependability, to take that risk. But now that he was mired back in the muck of his life, he didn't know what to do. He felt as if a trick had been played on him. He wanted to return to the clarity, but was fearful the old men wouldn't be able to fix him again. Maybe he was even more fearful they could fix him and then he'd have to go through these up-and-down cycles again. It felt like being plunged through the waves, one moment breathing and the next drowning, then back again. He remembered tumbling through the river and the feeling of suffocation as he fought for air. It seemed like more torture than he could bear to be back in the middle of the pain in the wake of knowing some peace and a bit of joy.

With resignation he realized he had nothing left to lose and had no clear alternative other than to return to the old men. Very early in the morning when the two weeks were up, he climbed back in his truck and drove down the mountain along Dry Creek, back up the mountain along the main fork of the Kaweah, then up along the East Fork toward the cabin.

MARIA
March 2009

When Maria first discovered she was pregnant she felt a mixture of fear and warm gladness. She was going to tell JR, but as time went on she decided it wasn't a good idea. She knew him well enough to know that he'd try to do the right thing out of obligation, but she wasn't looking for someone to be with her and her child out of begrudging obligation. He wouldn't be able to maintain the relationship for the long haul anyway, what with his demons and all. She didn't even consider an abortion as life was too sacred to her and she'd dedicated her life to bringing new life into the world. She didn't know how she could make it, but she believed somehow she'd find a way.

She left without a word, because there weren't any words that could suffice. A note said she was leaving and that was it.

Maria didn't hate JR or blame him for the situation. She loved him, but she knew she couldn't save him from his hell and she didn't want her child to have to also live through the effects of that hell. He was a good man underneath it all, but it was one thing to sleep with a troubled man and imagine some different romantic outcome and quite another to introduce an innocent child into some dream she might have of how things could be. Her child would need the security of the reality of love, not a fantasy of it coupled with grudging obligation.

After she left JR, Maria found a small farmhouse down in the valley where she was surrounded by all the dividing branches of the river. The house was set back in the middle of a grove of walnut trees. On summer evenings after the long hot days she walked along the sandy riverbanks. In early summer she waded through the water until the time it all dried up from heat and irrigation usage.

Maria's mother came to help when the baby was born and still dropped in occasionally. Maria came from a lineage of Mexican farmworkers, but her mother's mother had been Indian, a Wukchumne. Though Maria had watched her grandmother weave traditional baskets and even helped her gather the grasses and reeds, Maria never embraced the native traditions. When she wove the baskets Maria felt something stir and it scared her. There was something within the old place in her that was so deeply sad that she didn't want to touch it – she couldn't touch it. Her grandmother watched her without saying much. Maria would have to come to it in her own time.

Maria forged ahead through school on her quest to become a nurse and endured the taunts of the other girls who daily tried to keep each other in line and corralled into sameness and ignorance. All they wanted was a boyfriend, then babies. Maria wanted a man, but she also wanted more. After she'd been a delivery nurse for a while she became a midwife. When she returned to the valley, Maria took a steady nursing job in Visalia so she could provide for Sophia and use the health benefits.

While she was growing up, Maria assumed her parents had a perfect relationship until one day her dad left. Overnight, Maria, her sister, and her mom were on their own. Maria began to dream of establishing her own perfect relationship to offset the pain of losing her father. She dreamed of meeting the special someone and feeling the magic. She dreamed of being married and having children of her own.

"Maybe I'm not any different than the girls in high school."

The thought depressed her, but she could only try dreaming of something better.

She dreamed of finding a man who would stay, a man she could count on.

Her search had been rocky and led to a number of bad relationships. Some had been abusive, but she clung to the hope that the spark in the sex could be fanned into something more intimate, romantic, and enduring.

JR hadn't been abusive, but he drank too much. Her inclination was to try to heal whatever she could, but she knew the pain he carried was beyond her capacity to heal. It was difficult for her to distinguish between the situations where she could truly provide some healing and those where it was only an exercise in futility and wasted energy. If JR was going to be whole – and their relationship solid – it would take a miracle from someone else or somewhere else. She knew she couldn't be the everything and he couldn't be the everything. There was no future to it, so she left.

Maria was surprised when JR showed up at her door, but she always knew the day would come. It was fortunate he happened to come by on one of her days off. When she invited him in, Maria didn't know what to say.

For once Maria was glad JR didn't try to say much. She usually was trying to get him to say something about how he felt, but now she wouldn't have known how to keep a conversation alive. When he leaned over to kiss her goodbye, she sensed that something had happened to him, something deep and profound. She wanted to kiss him back, but stopped herself.

JR went out the front door and past the hydran-gea bushes toward his truck. Maria clutched her daughter tightly.

Things had seemed clear before and now they weren't.

Elements of Being iii

It could be said that space is the warp and time is the weft of this reality, the fabric of space-time shot through with holes of the timeless. Or, it could be said that this is all a frothing brew, the glistening bubbles of reality wrapped around cores of timeless void, our faces and the ten-thousand things, mirrored to us many times over on the shimmering surface of existence.

Wu Jiyan

THE CRYING DANCE
March 2009

The cabin seemed to swim into view when he drove up the road, suddenly emerging into JR's consciousness as if from a mist. The old men were out by the creek working in their garden when they heard the approaching truck. They put down their tools and circled around the cabin to meet him. JR didn't quite know what to say, though inside he felt ready to explode. All he could do was stick out his hand and say, "Hello, again."

Wu invited him into the cabin.

"Would you like some tea?"

JR nodded as he looked warily around the room trying to spot Wu's stick. He certainly didn't want to be caught by any surprises. Wu's lips formed a half-smile of amusement while Francisco laughed at JR's concern.

The tea seemed to calm JR enough that he could muster a few thoughts and words.

"Look, there's a few things I've got to understand...," he started, but found himself cut off by Francisco.

"Finish your tea, then we'll take a walk. One thing, then the other."

After the tea Wu gestured toward the door, picked up his staff and guided them outside. JR eyed the stick.

"You going to hit me with that thing?"

Wu laughed. "You can't do that very often. If you use the stick too much, then the poor guy would have no insides left."

Francisco joined in.

"We'd have to stuff you with tules or straw, but then you wouldn't be a human being anymore."

JR looked blankly at the laughing Francisco. He hadn't paid much attention to the old men's voices before this moment, since they hadn't spoken much. Wu's voice sounded a bit Chinese, but it was inflected with the sounds of JR's own Okie speech. Francisco's voice carried some kind of Indian rhythm, but JR could also hear Mexican as well as Okie in it.

They began to walk and JR wondered again who the old guys were.

He was concerned about how far they'd be walking and whether he'd have to climb through rocks. He was wearing his old cowboy boots and they'd slip and slide on rocks, especially near the water. The old guys seemed pretty spry.

They headed uphill and followed a trail through the trees, then after about a mile the trail neared the creek where they had to cross. The area around the creek was strewn with large boulders that created dams for the water. The water formed deep pools then cascaded over the rocks in small waterfalls. JR had to watch his step while he hopped from boulder to boulder, wary of the slippery green moss. On the other side the trail ascended again until they came out on a flattened knoll fringed by oak and manzanita interspersed with blooming redbud trees. From there he could look down to the canyon of the East Fork and see waterfalls and stretches of whitewater. It was still early enough in the morning that the sun hadn't quite crested the mountains behind them and the men still stood in shadow

The old men sat down on two of the boulders and gestured for JR to also sit. JR felt a strange compulsion to tell them about his pain. He tried to tell them about his daddy and him going and killing himself, about his daddy and Vietnam, about himself and the suffering and misery of Iraq, and how he felt he was going to explode. He didn't even know how to tell them about how he craved his daddy's love and how he'd been made to feel like shit and how he wished his daddy were still here even though he hated him. He never made it to Maria and Sophia.

It was like he'd taken another big shit in front of them.

The old men looked at JR solemnly and reached out to touch his hands for a few moments. Then they laughed. The laughter shocked JR into awareness. It wasn't mocking laughter or pitying laughter. It was a laughter that JR couldn't place within his experience. It was as if all creation was rolled into it and saying, "Yeah, ain't it a bitch." The laughter also contained depths of knowing that told him there was indeed far more if he was ready for it.

When the old men finished laughing they began to tell stories. Wu told JR of the tens of millions that had died around him in China. He told JR of the unwashed, ungodly British and of the man who thought he was Jesus's brother. When Wu finished, Francisco told how his own people had died of sickness, starvation, and greed. They finished talking and fell silent. They laughed again.

"Yeah, ain't it a bitch. Life is mysterious and hard, but there's more."

Suddenly, the laughter stopped. The old men began to cry and they cried for everything and everyone.

JR felt his heart torn apart as the old men wept, and he too began to cry for everything and everyone. The tears he felt and tasted weren't his familiar inner tears of frustration and rage at his own personal life, but for something larger. The tears washed him and fell to the ground.

While they all cried, Francisco got up and began to dance, a slow shuffling dance, and he began to chant in a language that JR couldn't recognize, but without being told he knew it was for the suffering and the dead. Wu rose from his rock and joined Francisco. They put their foreheads together and wrapped their arms about each other's shoulders and continued to dance, Francisco still chanting in his own native language and Wu chanting in Chinese.

JR felt an inexplicable compulsion to rise and join them. He moved toward Francisco and Wu and wrapped his arms around them, then touched his head to theirs as the strange words washed over him. In his mind he saw the faces of dead and maimed Iraqis and saw lines of ancestors that stretched behind them toward ancient garden cities along a great river in the desert. The faces all cried out for a peace they couldn't find. He saw his own ancestors stretched across a vast American landscape and he cried for these ancestors and the peace they couldn't find.

The light began to creep over the mountain and toward the three men and toward the tears that now glistened and watered the ground. The tears flowed in rivulets down the mountain toward the river.

After the three men disengaged from the crying dance they again sat on the boulders silently for a half hour, gazing out over the canyon. Francisco suddenly laughed to break the silence.

"That was a good one."

At the sound of the laughter, Wu rose and moved around, then leaned on his staff while he stretched.

"There are some things you need to know, but I can't show or tell you everything in one sitting. Besides, you somehow need to experience them if you can. I'll tell you this. Of the tremendous pain you experience, only a fraction of it is really yours. Your personal pain is up close and in your face, so that's all you see. Behind it is a vast field of pain, the pain of the blind and the dead who are living, the pain of all, and it reaches out and engulfs you even though you don't know it's there. You have to give up your personal complaints about life to deal with the larger issues of pain. You were free for a moment when you could dance in grief for everyone.

"We're in this together."

While Wu was speaking JR remembered his sense of being overcome by feelings that he couldn't even identify as his own, and of his body twitching in response to things he couldn't see or perceive. He knew there had to be more than what he was being told. JR tried to ask a question, but Francisco cut him off.

"All in due time. This isn't a lecture class. This isn't about theory. You can only learn what you're ready to take in, learn what you're ready to experience. We'll point you in a direction and try to fill in the gaps, but it's up to you to learn it. If I tell you a story and ask you to simply believe it, then you haven't learned anything. You don't know whether it's true or false and what you want to believe overrides any concerns about whether the story is true or false. Beliefs aren't fundamental reality. Beliefs are substitutes for reality and most people live their lives in their belief-ridden, sub-stitute-reality world. These substitute realities are propped up by personal pain and fear."

Francisco began stacking stones into a pile ten to twelve inches high. JR looked around and noticed other rock cairns in the area that formed a geometric figure. When Francisco finished, Wu pushed himself up with his staff and began moving down the hill toward the creek crossing while taking slow pleasure in the new morning light.

The three men walked silently back toward the cabin. When JR slipped on one of the rocks crossing the creek, Wu leaned on his staff to reach out and steady him. Back at the cabin, Wu walked to a wall cabinet and pulled out a loaf of coarse bread and a piece of dried meat, then set about fanning embers in the stove so he could heat water for tea. In the meantime Francisco went to the creek and retrieved a hunk of cheese from a watertight box set in the water. When the water was heated and tea brewed, the three men sat outside on upturned tree sections and ate their lunch.

JR broke finally broke the silence.

"Why did I meet you…why am I here?"

"The mountains and rivers brought you to us," replied Wu, "and we don't know anything more than that, at least for now."

The men went back to their tea and food in silence.

JR tried for a few moments to figure out Wu's enigmatic reply, then went inward. He studied the silence that enfolded his mind and body and watched streams of energy, feelings, and faces course by without pulling him into their current. He didn't know how long this peace would last, but he wanted to savor it as long as possible. He found a momentary end to the incessant voices of his desires. The silence was interrupted by an old memory. He was a boy working in a field down in the flatland with a middle-aged Okie. The man told JR the story about his own daddy, an old man in his seventies who'd gotten cancer in his balls and had to have them cut off. The old man was suddenly free of the compulsion that had driven him most of his life. The experience of silence and freedom so overwhelmed him that he told his son that if he'd known how peaceful it was, he'd have had the goddamn things cut off long ago. JR realized that he hadn't wanted to be rid of his own compulsions and obsessions, as painful as they might be. He was sure that whoever or whatever he thought he was, for good or bad, would disappear, and he'd simply be a hollow, empty bag of skin. He hadn't been able to imagine who he could possibly be without the desire and pain to define him.

When Wu struck him with the staff on his first visit, JR was overwhelmed for a long time and not nearly clearheaded enough to contemplate everything in detail. Now, JR felt a great clarity and presence. He hadn't disappeared and he wasn't an empty bag of skin, but he wasn't quite sure who or what he was.

Francisco watched as JR searched through the silence of his mind.

"You have to develop a self, a real self, otherwise you're just a shit bag of impulses with hardly a glimmer of what it takes to be a real human being," Francisco said. "Religious folks are always telling you how bad the self is and how you should give it up or annihilate it or that it's an illusion, but you need a real self. They tell you that so it's easier to control you. Your self is not your pain or your habits or your desires, it's not your learning or things you own, and it's not what you're told to believe you are. Until you find your real self you aren't a full human being. You need to find an essence that doesn't need to invent excuses for its existence and doesn't need to invent beliefs or rules or excuses to justify itself. That self is what can observe your pain and the pain of the world and sort it out and keep it at a safe distance."

"You told me that only a part of the pain I felt was really mine," said JR. "What do you mean by that?"

"We share a collective mind," said Wu. "If you don't watch it, you'll be overcome by the pain of everyone around you. Your self is what regulates how much to let in for your survival. The poor folks you call crazy have no real self and they're living in the constant storm of the world's pain and fear. Telling them to have no self is condemning them to hell."

"Wouldn't it be best to find a way to just shut it all out, make it go away?" JR asked.

"No," said Wu. "You'd never get to the deepest parts of your being and you'd never find your compassion, and without compassion you'd simply be an empty, ravenous, mindless being. The insanity of the world is near the surface and you have to learn to dive through it to get to the light at the bottom of the ocean. You have to live in relationship with the world's pain and let it teach you, let it guide you to wisdom and understanding."

The old men remained silent for the rest of the afternoon while they worked around the cabin, digging the earth and chopping wood. When they began to put the tools away, JR remembered the question he'd wanted to ask.

"How old are you guys?"

"Over two hundred years," Wu replied. He turned back to sharpening tools and putting them away without further explanation.

After dinner the old men told JR he should stay for the night. He pulled his sleeping bag from the truck, rolled it out on the ground and watched the stars overhead until he fell asleep.

JR awoke to a radio blaring, but there was no discernible type of sound, just grating, cacophonous noise. It seemed like all the frequencies were coming in at once with wavelengths piling over the top of each other in mounting frenzy. He heard snatches of voices and felt his body respond in various uncontrollable ways to the sounds. Anxiety and fear ran through his body like electrical currents, while the voices from the radio seemed to compel him to random action. He felt like a dead frog hooked to a battery, twitching uncontrollably. He looked down along his body and saw a golden control knob protruding from his belly. He reached down to touch the knob. He turned it and the frequencies separated into discernible patterns. He heard conversations and ramblings as well as pure terror and the sound of music. If he wanted to, he could make sense of any strand of the sounds coming from the radio. He also found he could turn down the volume, but it never went away. He simply managed the noise.

The old men smiled in their sleep. Things were becoming clearer.

In the morning JR woke to a shuffling, dragging sound punctuated by a low growl. He rolled over to see a mountain lion dragging a deer carcass across the ground about twenty feet from him. The lion eyed him briefly, let out another muffled growl, then dragged the deer toward the door of the cabin. The door opened and the old men stepped out. They spoke a few words to the animal and the lion swished its tail a few times in response. The lion turned and retraced its path toward the trees then lay down near the base of one of the oaks.

Francisco went back into the cabin for a moment and returned with a knife. He quickly removed a haunch from the deer while Wu chanted a prayer of thanksgiving. After he finished, Francisco dragged the body back in the direction of the lion. The lion rose and met Francisco halfway across the clearing, then paused for a moment as both old men spoke to her in gratitude. When the men finished speaking, the lion pulled the carcass back toward the trees. The lion vocalized a few soft calls and two half-grown cubs came out of the brush to join her. The cats began to feed.

JR had seen lions in the wild, though they were elusive. At times JR knew he was being watched, but never knew from where. He'd just never seen them up close. He wondered if this was the source of yesterday's dried meat.

The lions ignored him, so JR quickly grabbed his sleeping bag and walked into the cabin where Francisco stood at a counter slicing the meat into strips

He still had a lot of questions, especially about the night's dream. He also had no clue what to do about Maria and Sophia. Francisco finished what he was doing, rinsed his hands at the sink, and walked over to JR.

"See you again in two weeks."

Francisco gestured toward the door.

JR walked out to his truck and at each step looked around for the lions. The cats – and the deer – were gone. JR knew the deer was probably somewhere nearby covered with leaves, hidden for another visit.

JR climbed into his truck and headed down the dirt road.

About a half-mile from the cabin he passed a short Mexican man walking along the road. He had long hair and a beard, and tattoos peeked out above his shirt collar and below his shirtsleeves. JR continued driving. He didn't notice the man trip in a pothole and fall after the truck had passed. The man held his ankle and moaned, sure that he was doomed.

THE SERMON

Padre Serra looked out over the faces of the parishioners before him in the dimly lit church. Some were soldiers, but most were local Indians and mestizos who had given up their old ways and joined the Church. They had given up their fanciful and sometimes colorful ways of dress from the past and wore simple white to observe the Mass. It was best this way, the padre thought, to remove all color until there was only the black-and-white certainty of God's will. Color was merely a distraction in the effort to know God's certainty and bow before it. Color was a distraction behind which sin could hide.

The padre paid little attention to the color and detail of the world as he walked through it, preferring to keep his mind focused on the rosary or some other form of prayer. That was how he'd ignored the detail of the snake in his path. He didn't allow himself the slightest bit of enjoyment and never allowed a smile to frame his lips – lips that should only form the words of prayers and sermons. He knew nothing of science or art and kept himself willfully ignorant of any challenge to his certainty.

The padre stood toward the head of the cross that formed the mission chapel and tried to decide what he could say to inspire the mestizos and Indios before him to strive for greater and greater spiritual attainment. When he stepped forward to speak at the pulpit, he let his habit fall from his shoulders, and exposed his scarred chest, deformed from beatings with rocks and whips, burned with flaming sticks.

Padre Serra began to beat himself with a chain, all the while exhorting the faithful in front of him to greater penance before God. He beat himself repeatedly and without mercy, and moved the worshippers to tears.

One of the parishioners stepped forward from congregation, took the chains from the good father's hands, stripped to his waist, and began to beat his own body in vicious emulation of the padre.

"I am the sinner, ungrateful to God, who ought to do penance for my many sins, and not the father who is a saint."

The man flailed himself over and over as the padre watched in spiritual awe.

The man beat himself until he fell to the floor and was silent, no longer moving. Padre Serra knelt by the man, bent forward to touch the devout soul, and administered the last unction and sacrament before the weeping, wailing crowd.

The man died within a few hours.

In the face of such deep piety Padre Serra felt compelled to raise his own level of penance for sins both known and unknown. He still worked to strip away everything until he could find the core sin of his being and assure his eternal salvation.

THE CURRENT
March 2009

JR swung off the saddle and dismounted his horse near the creek. It had been a week since he'd been part of the crying dance with Wu and Francisco and he was still in a quandary. His life had turned upside down. Not only did he have to figure out how to be a father, but he also had to deal with the situation with the old men, which every rational sense told him was impossible. It brought up memories of being in the church while he was growing up. Even though the church didn't much factor into how he dealt with things anymore, he could hear sermons echoing in his head, telling him he was wrong again, always wrong, and that this whole strange affair was the work of the devil. What he did know is that even though he'd only seen the old men a few times, it seemed like they were genuinely concerned about him. For JR, it was a new experience. The old men seemed to see him at a deeper level than anyone he'd ever met, and without a hint of judgment.

When JR was in relationships, he always kept a big part of himself in reserve because he knew if the woman really knew everything about him she'd be horrified. It was also true of any friendship. These old men knew everything about him and didn't care. They saw who he was before his daddy had beat him down with words and a belt. They saw who he was before he'd fucked up his life in ways he could never confess to anyone. For some reason he was more than a goddamn peckerwood to them. He had no clear idea why the old men had been there to pull him from the river, but he was deeply appreciative.

JR left his horse to graze on the spring grasses for a few minutes while he went down to the creek. There were a few shallow pools hollowed out in the granite where the water slowly flowed through in the sunlight. JR remembered his first experience at the cabin and how the old men had put him in the creek. He took off his clothes, walked into the water and splashed himself a few times before he lay down in one of the pools. The water was cool but bearable. Upstream the creek widened and flowed shallow over a rocky bed, allowing the sun to warm the water a bit. Laying back in the sunlight also helped. He felt the slow current pull around his body.

After the crying dance, the sense of peace stayed with him for four or five days. The crying temporarily emptied a deep dark reservoir that never before had an outlet. The peace began to slip away as JR tried to re-enter his world. He knew he wanted to find that feeling again, no matter what it took, and he felt compelled to look for it in the same way he used to look for sex.

JR let himself relax further into the water. The current seemed to pull his anguish and fear into the water and carry it away. Maybe he'd found a way to help himself a bit. He wasn't one to just stretch out in the creek, though he'd waded in it and jumped off high rocks into it, but he'd never just let himself lie down in the water. After a bit he pulled himself from the water and walked up to a polished slab of exposed granite and stretched out on the stone, oblivious to the hard surface. He seemed to sink into the rock, cushioned by the intermingling of his molecules with that of the granite.

As he lay back, JR looked around at the infinite shades of springtime green and the wildflowers pushing through. He looked at the trees – the ceanothus and the redbud – and he could feel the colors and shapes and textures take over his mind more than they ever had before. It stirred something so deep within that he wanted to express it, but he didn't know how, and the frustration at being unable to express the sensory deluge threatened to overwhelm him.

JR thought of his experience in the creek a few minutes before and imagined how it had felt lying back in the water. When he did so, the imaginary water began to pull the frustration away. The frustration parted like a veil and in the mind-current he saw his daughter's face framed by bronze hair. Then he saw Maria.

JR had wanted the old men to tell him what to do about Sophia and Maria, but had never been able to ask the question. Now he knew with calm certainty what to do. Maria and his daughter were part of the color and shape of the world that he needed to express, even though he didn't know how to do it. He'd have to learn.

JR gathered up his clothes, dressed, and walked over to his horse. He stepped into the stirrup, swung his leg over the saddle and headed upstream. He had more cattle to look for before he could head back home.

SCOURGED

Francisco had come to peace with as many things as he could about the ways of the people in the valley below him. He'd forgiven as much of it as he could over the long cycle of his time on the planet. Francisco still had trouble with priests though, and he didn't know when he'd ever be able to resolve it. He had little trouble with the notion of Jesus, though he couldn't understand how any part of the universe could be any more a part of God than another. It was all one piece, all Great Mind, even into the time-less. Francisco knew that someday he'd run into this Jesus in one of his visions or on a walk into the high mountains. Priests were another matter entirely. Francisco's deformed thumb bore mute testimony to the effects of the priests' love and he still shuddered when he remembered the interminable forced kneeling in the dark buildings where he was made to sing praises of gratitude for being a slave. Francisco still felt a great anger toward Padre Serra for creating the missions that destroyed Francisco's original family and tribe, and nearly destroyed him.

It was said the Padre Serra didn't know, or want to know, what pleasure was – certainly not the grace of a woman or the beauty of a child. He couldn't appreciate a tree, the dawn, or the curving arc of a river through the mountains. The padre insisted that everyone else feel his pain at having a body and having a life. Francisco knew from his own experience that life brought enough pain in its natural course without the need to add to it. Willfully adding more pain on top of pain seemed a desecration of life.

The padre was a crippled man, crippled and scourged, a way of life he'd forced on the Indian people, a condition that became the Indian way of life – crippled and scourged. The thought that the Church could consider the man for sainthood without a hint of apology was sometimes almost more than Francisco could bear. It was just another reason to stay in the mountains with Wu. He knew if he were in the Middle Ages he'd be burned. In fact there were moments when he closed his eyes that he could see himself tied to a stake with bundles of branches piled around. He could see a hooded priest set the bundles on fire and could feel the intense pain as he breathed in the acrid wood smoke mixed with the smell of his own burning flesh. He didn't know if he was remembering another life he'd lived, or whether he was experiencing the life of someone else in the collective web of memories. Or, maybe it was just a metaphor for the destruction of his old life. Francisco felt betrayed by the priests and believed the priests had desecrated the deepest possible meaning of life.

Sometimes when he was in the vision world or in a dream, Francisco encountered his personal demon, and the demon always wore the face of Padre Serra. In one hand the demon carried a staff in the form of the serpent, the serpent that struck the padre in the foot and shriveled his leg. In the other hand he carried a scourge of knotted rope embedded with sharp bits of glass. The demon chastised Francisco and told him he must flail himself mercilessly, and if Francisco didn't do it, the demon would beat him instead. It was all for Francisco's own salvation. When that happened, Francisco prayed to be able to forgive the Church and its priests, but it had never happened.

Francisco was conscious of his failures. Even after all the intervening years, he still thought of John Wood and wished for some absolution. It wasn't something he could casually forget or forgive. It was in these moments that Padre Serra appeared in order to flog and scourge him for his sin. The padre and Wood were points of personal pain beyond which he hadn't been able to move. Francisco could go for long periods of time without being assaulted by this personal pain, but there were moments when it came forth in a full fury aimed at destroying his sense of being. Francisco knew he needed to resolve his personal pain before he died, because if he didn't, he'd trip on the unresolved things when he tried to cross the river. It had existed this way for nearly 200 years, yet he knew it could be lifted in a moment. In the meantime he could only watch and wait with all the awareness he could muster and not allow the regret and guilt to flail him into mindlessness and unconsciousness.

In the moments when Padre Serra appeared to Francisco, Wu would laugh and threaten to use his stick on Francisco, but both men knew the time wasn't yet right. Francisco would simply have to let the demon be and go about its business while watching its every move for an opening. Direct combat with the demon was impossible. It would only cause great damage to the both of them without any conclusion. The only solution was unending patience.

Watch and wait. Watch and see.

There was one great difference between Francisco and Wu. Wu had never had a family – no wife, no children. In fact, Wu had been a celibate for most of his life, except for a few occasions when he was a young man. He could still remember an encounter with a young prostitute. He was a shy young man with no social skill and his parents had no money or social standing to arrange a good match. He'd fumbled his way through the encounter while the woman had done the best she could to guide him. He could still remember the keen pleasure of touching her body and disappearing, but afterward he devoted himself to his studies and his imperial exams.

Over the course of his spiritual search, his experiences of the deeper world became more profound than his experiences of sex. He found no reason to go back and explore the sexual world again. Besides that, the great upheavals – the Opium Wars and the Taiping Rebellion – and his need for survival, overwhelmed any sexual thoughts he had.

Francisco still missed his wife and son, even after all the years. He also missed village life and the connections between every member of the tribe. Sorrow was not a bad thing. It was a measure of respect for the good aspects of life, respect for things that brought joy in their time before passing on. Francisco wondered if Padre Serra ever knew the celebration that is sorrow, the respect for things that brought joy during their brief temporal stay. The expression of proper sorrow left an opening for some new encounter with happiness or joy, an elevation from the bumps and pains of having a body and having a life.

Francisco also knew for certain that if you stopped and truly appreciated the temporal reality of a tree, a mountain, or a river, you couldn't scourge your mind and your body at the same time.

FLIGHT
April 2009

JR looked around at his unfamiliar surroundings and realized he was walking along an unlit
street with a storm building all about him. When the
wind buffeted his body and pelted him with rain, a
primal joy began to move through his entire being
and propel him to run faster and faster through the
elements. He wasn't running to escape the storm. He
was running to exult in the raw feeling of the energy.
He wasn't afraid of being exposed to the full power
of the elements and reveled in the freedom from fear.
JR ran even faster, then raised his arms and began to
move them up and down. He wore a dark coat with
loose sleeves that caught the wind as he moved his
arms. JR rose above the ground as his arms and coat
sleeves transformed into black wings that pushed
against the air. He was a giant black raven in the
night sky. He knew he was dreaming, but the dream
was as real as anything he'd ever experienced. In the
past JR had flown in dreams, but he was simply like
a kite or balloon unable to maneuver, blown about
by wind and circumstance. The lack of control
scared him as each gust of wind or downdraft felt

like he was falling off the edge of a cliff. JR pressed down with his wings and flew higher through the wind and rain and dark clouds without wavering, no longer buffeted by the storm. He emerged above the clouds with the primal energy still pulsing through his mind and through his wings, and began to soar in circles above the storm. He scanned the skies looking for others, but could see no one else.

He knew he'd have to land on the ground some-time, but he had enough energy to stay aloft above the storm and last it out.

JR awoke. There was light coming through the windows but the sun still hadn't risen over the moun-tains. He vividly remembered the flying and the exhilaration and power he felt while piercing through the storm. He also remembered the loneliness he felt as he circled above the storm and found no one else to share the sky. It brought back waves of feeling starkly alone throughout his life. He had always been alone in a storm, buffeted and battered by the forces at hand. His new power of flight enlivened him, but he wanted to fly with others. The two old men had each other, but JR didn't know if he could be an ongoing part of their lives for any length of time.

There was also a snippet of dream that JR barely remembered. He was standing in front of the foun-dations of a house he was to build. Trouble was he wasn't a carpenter and didn't know how to build houses. The plans he held in his hand were blank sheets of paper.

The flying energy moved through JR's body as he got up from bed. He pulled on an old shirt and pants and walked outside to sit on a rock. He breathed in the fresh morning air and watched the sun light the higher reaches of the mountains above him. Patches of color leaped out of the shadows as the sun reached the flowering trees on the slopes. JR decided he'd have to head to the valley and talk with Maria soon. He couldn't keep going it alone, even with the profundity of his new experiences.

It was strange he'd yearned to be close to other people his whole life, but when he got close he always felt burned and abused. Now he needed others flying with him, yet he didn't even know if Maria wanted to, or was up to the task. Besides that, he knew she wouldn't be enough by herself. JR didn't know how he'd present himself to Maria or tell her what was going on without sounding crazy. He was afraid of failing and being a goddamn fool again, but he had to try.

REPOSE
August 1784

Padre Serra lay dying, clutching for breath. His battered and scarred chest tried to expand and pull in more air, but the slightest movement brought a spasm of pain that stopped the attempt. He tried to keep his mind still and focused on God, and as he did so he began to feel a surety slowly creep through his being. This, finally, was the fruit of all his penance and discipline. Around him several priests prayed as one of them performed the last rites.

He stood by a turbulent river and before him was a bridge. The place where he stood was in a deep shadow, but on the other side of the river the sun shone brightly. Across the water he could make out a gated golden city on the horizon that seemed brighter than the daylight. The city protruded from a barren desert landscape that contained no signs of earthly life, but the city was all that mattered. He was drawn toward the bridge and to the promise of the heavenly realm.

Padre Serra approached the bridge, but as he did the bridge rapidly narrowed. He began to chant the rosary. Remembering his experience of the snakebite, he tried to bring his attention to each footstep. Without warning, his memories of the pain he'd inflicted upon himself over a lifetime struck with full force. The memories smashed into his body like an enormous scourge and carried him off the narrow beam that was now the bridge, and into the whitewater below. When the current grabbed him, the haunting fear behind the condemned faces in the paintings from his youth began to swirl through his mind. He remembered the bruja woman in Mexico whom he sent to the Inquisition and how she died in prison. Her dirty wild-eyed face haunted him and she loudly called forth the faces of Indios and mestizos whose bodies were wounded and bloodied by the large crucifix he held in his hand like a sword. He was disoriented by the turbulent rush of faces – faces that cried out to him for compassion and justice. His mind was a chaos, the very chaos he'd worked to avoid. The chaos exposed his inadequacy before God, the inadequacy he'd tried to strip away from his earthly mind and body.

Padre Serra was tumbled, scourged, and beaten by the force of the whitewater and the faces until he fell into a repose of prayer and waiting. He tried to form a green candle in his mind and to hold an image of heaven before his eyes. His world slowed to infinite nothing and he dwelt beyond hope or prayer.

FOUR
April 2009

Maria was surprised when JR showed up at the door. She didn't think he'd own up to things and follow through on his promise to come back. He didn't do much talking, though. He said he couldn't explain what was happening and would have to show her.

"I have to think about it. I can't just run off on your whim."

She was just starting a rotation of three days off. She had the time, but she had to understand why. Maria invited him into the house. The moment he walked through the door Sophia came up to him and took his hand as Maria watched closely. After holding JR's hand for a few seconds Sophia reached up to indicate she wanted to be held. At that moment Maria knew she'd go with JR, but didn't say anything.

They went for a walk on one of the sandy roads along the riverbank and afterward Maria fixed dinner while JR played awkwardly with Sophia in the living room. Maria was baffled and didn't know what to make of JR's actions. He was certainly behaving differently than he had in the past.

After dinner Maria and JR played with Sophia until the child tired, then put her to bed. They sat on the couch, leaning back against a saddle blanket that JR once gave her. She'd sometimes gone riding with him on one of his boss's extra horses and he'd given her the blanket. It was handwoven and hand-dyed in shades of lavenders, roses, reds, and purples by some lady over in Three Rivers. He'd tried to tell Maria about how underneath all his pain that the colors were how he really saw the world, that he wanted her to be the colors. JR also gave her a pair of green malachite earrings that he said went with her dark hair. She hadn't worn them much between work and raising a child.

She and JR sat on the couch for a while, then began kissing in the old way and stripping away each other's clothes. When she sat astride him, with him leaning back against the blanket, he melted. He simply held her and she felt his tears rolling down her breasts. They sat in the embrace until she took his hand and led him off to bed.

In the morning Maria called her mother to see if she could come and get Sophia, then dressed for the day. On a whim she put on the dark green earrings. After her mother arrived, Maria and JR left in his truck.

They made their way up the dirt road toward the old men's cabin and Maria didn't know what to expect. JR had said something about two old men and that one was Chinese and the other was some kind of Indian. She couldn't get much more out of him except that if he said any more she'd think he was crazy.

JR parked in front of the cabin and the old men came out from behind the building. Maria noticed that the cabin seemed to meld into the landscape as if it were part of it, as if some care had been taken in its placement and construction. It wasn't a ramshackle wart like most old cabins she'd seen. The two men walked up and JR introduced them. As she was being introduced to Francisco he looked into her eyes and suddenly questioned her.

"What tribe are you?"

Maria was caught off-guard. No one ever asked about her Indian heritage. Scarcely anyone knew. "My grandmother is Wukchumne."

"Not just Wukchumne, you're Kaweah."

Maria didn't know what to make of Francisco's response. She didn't know anything about the Kaweah, other than it was the name of the river. It seemed the name must also be that of a tribe. She heard a raven laugh in a distant tree.

Wu leaned on a staff of manzanita with a carving of a face at the top. When Francisco finished, Wu spoke.

"About time there was a woman here to learn things. What kept you?"

Wu chuckled.

"The green is a good sign," gesturing toward her ears.

The old men led her into the cabin where Wu began to fix some tea. Maria sipped her tea and watched the old men. Francisco suddenly leaned over and looked her in the eye.

"Romantic notions blind you!"

"Blind me to what?"

Wu interjected.

"This isn't romantic, this is real."

He began to pound the floor with his stick and shook the carved face in front of her. The floor reverberated.

"Don't be complacent!"

Maria's mind reeled. The old men had gone crazy and now she no longer felt safe. They began to dance wildly around her. Why had she'd come to this place? She felt like a fool for listening to JR.

She looked over at JR for help, but he didn't show any concern.

She became angry.

She rarely allowed herself to feel anger since she was always smoothing things over. She was angry that her father had left, angry that she hadn't gotten what she'd imagined for herself in life, angry that she hadn't been swept away with love, angry that she was a single parent, angry that no one had rescued her from her situation, angry that trying to think all the right things had gotten her nowhere, and now she was angry at JR for allowing the crazy old men to torment her.

The moment Maria's anger reached a peak that verged on volcanic explosion, Francisco placed his hand on her shoulder.

Suddenly it was over.

The anger flowed out of her body through his hand, bringing a sense of calm. She hadn't even been aware that such anger existed in her depths. She observed her fears beneath the anger, like looking down through clear water, and it all suddenly seemed ridiculous.

She laughed. She couldn't help herself. She danced around herself in laughter.

Francisco made motions as if he were galloping up on a horse.

"No white knights, no castles in the air!"

Wu shook the staff in front of Maria's face again. When he did, the carved face appeared to smile for an instant. The swirling wood grain of deep red and weathered silver gray seemed to contain everything she needed to know. She was pulled into Dizang's eyes.

Maria laughed again and the old men laughed with her. Maria looked over at JR watching her bemusedly. She couldn't tell if he really understood all she'd just experienced. She wanted to tell him, but knew she couldn't, so she settled back into the joy of the moment – there in the cabin at the edge of the flowing creek on the surface of the earth beneath the unseen stars of day.

A voice broke her reverie.

"Should have seen what that one went through," Francisco said, gesturing in JR's direction.

"Took a long time to clean that one up," Wu chimed in. He made mopping motions with his stick. Both of the old men looked in JR's direction, then doubled over in laughter.

JR smiled, embarrassed.

"Look," said Francisco, "if you want to be together, you have to be willing to experience what really is, together, without illusion."

Francisco gestured in JR's direction.

"He can't live in illusion any longer. If he does, it'll kill him. If he tries to live out your illusion, it'll kill him. You have to be willing to give up illusion if you want to be with him and have him survive. You have to give up what you want life to be in order to experience the mystery and power of what it really is. If you can do that, you'll find what you really need."

At the notion of giving up her desires, Maria felt her fear begin to rise.

Wu spoke. "JR's life has led him to a serious place and he has no choice about the conditions under which he lives, other than to give up illusion or die. You have a choice though. You could go on living in illusion for a long time, maybe lifetimes, before things got serious for you and you had no choice about it. You have to choose whether you follow him across the line into fundamental reality. If you can't do that, you should walk away for both your sakes."

Wu stopped for a moment, and Francisco picked up the thought.

"Life isn't a big piñata that we whack at and if we're lucky we get all the sweet things we desire. The Great Mind doesn't give a shit about your desires. Your desires are useless in the big scheme of things. What's important is to give up the fog of illusion created by your fear and desires so the Great Mind can see clearly through your eyes. If the Great Mind is able to do that, then it can see clearly what you need for your survival. You're important and valuable in the scheme of things if your eyes and your mind are clear. If they aren't clear, then most of your life is spent battered by random chance and staggering from encounter to encounter blinded by the fear that breeds your desires."

Wu drifted away while Francisco was speaking and came back with more hot tea. "It's good for sharpening the mind," he said, and poured the liquid into her cup.

When Maria finished the tea, she sat silently for a few minutes. Francisco came over and took her hand. He led her outside along the creek to a point where they could sit on boulders and talk. Before she could sit down, Francisco came up to her and pressed his forehead against hers.

Maria saw the faces of Yokuts – many, many Yokuts. She could feel them in her and she could see them weeping and crying for their dead. She saw bodies piling up too fast to properly mourn and the bodies being pushed into pits. She saw Francisco mourning over a woman and a child, and she saw crying women and children hauled off in wagons as men on horseback tracked down anyone who ran. She saw her people hunted for sport.

Maria wept and collapsed on the rock for support.

Francisco touched her head with his hand. "These are your people. They didn't do anything to deserve this. They didn't think bad thoughts or not enough good ones. Sometimes even when you do the best you can the shit will overrun you. The issue is whether you can meet your fate with as much dignity and clarity as you can. Some of us carried our dignity and some of us didn't. I didn't do so well at first."

Maria had never felt a connection to her Yokuts heritage, other than admiring her grandmother's baskets, and now she felt completely overwhelmed by sorrow. She understood why she'd avoided learning things from her grandmother. The depth of loss would have been too much to bear.

"You are crying for all those who came before you. It's a huge responsibility to be alive and to touch the Great Mind. Don't blind yourself with your silly notions."

Maria cried to the depths of her being. When she finished, Francisco led her back to the cabin.

COYOTE FALLS
April 2009

JR walked with Wu and Francisco across the bridge at Paradise Creek. In the middle he stopped and gazed downstream while his mind spun in endless circles trying to understand the night he'd been tossed over the railing into the water. Despite his confusion, he couldn't imagine his life without falling into the water and into the arms of the old men. Past the bridge they veered right and walked along the creek to the falls.

They followed the creek a short bit above the falls, making their way past the budding alder and other new growth along the creek bank until they came upon the body of a coyote lying next to the stream. It was a female who'd died giving birth, the first pup wedged sideways and unable to exit the womb. The mother must have sought water for her agony as the birth stalled and failed.

The old men looked closely and recognized the coyote as the mate of the one who'd brought them the rabbit. They both kneeled and offered a few words of blessing and then Francisco offered a little wild tobacco on her behalf.

JR was taken aback at the sight and felt unsettled. Memories of being at the falls with Maria washed through his mind – of how she'd risen up out of the water and he'd embraced her and they'd made love. The memory pressed against him like her body had, and he realized with a start that this was the place where Sophia was conceived.

JR pulled himself back into the present with the dead coyote and the old men. He didn't understand why they'd make offerings and pray over a coyote. He tried not to hate the animals, but he'd seen what they'd do to a calf if a pack of them had half a chance. It wasn't pretty and he'd been known to shoot a few in his day. Sometimes he had to take his anger out on something.

JR turned to Francisco.

"Why'd you do that?"

JR was surprised to notice how quickly his attitude had changed. One moment he was feeling a small measure of gratitude about the old men and the next moment he was feeling angry and shitty over the appearance of a dead coyote along the creek.

Francisco motioned for JR to come over next to the body. He took JR's hand and placed it on the coyote's belly near the pup that half protruded from her body.

"This is the entry point into the world and it's sad when life can't make it across. She and her mate were generous to us."

JR had witnessed bad births and stillborns with the cattle, but he didn't let himself feel a lot of concern, except for the economics of it. He'd already been torn up too much by dying and didn't want to think anything more about it.

The moment his hand touched the coyote's belly, JR thought of Sophia. She was conceived here along Paradise Creek and someday she was going to die. She could have died just like this, and Maria with her, and there was no telling when her time would actually come. JR never had many feelings about his own dying, and had sometimes desired it, but the thought of Sophia's death was more than he could bear. The sight and feel of the coyote overwhelmed him with grief and anger. He shouted at the old men.

"Why are you showing so much concern for a goddamn coyote? If it was still alive, would you try to save it?"

"Probably."

JR's anger rose. He felt insulted, diminished somehow. He certainly wanted Sophia to be more important than the dead coyote he was touching, didn't want her to end up a decaying body like all other decaying bodies. The coyotes would soon be crawling with maggots and so would Maria and Sophia.

Wu looked JR in the eyes for a moment.

"You're taking this personally aren't you? You want to be special. You don't like the thought of us treating this coyote with the same care and concern we treated you."

JR felt a jolt of electricity through his hand and jerked it away from the coyote's belly. Anguish seared through his body and he was gripped by insignificance and futility. He was overwhelmed by the immensity and profusion of life all around him and the sheer numbers of insects and animals and other unseen things fucking and shitting and dying. He felt lost and infinitely small.

A hand touched his forehead.

"The only specialness of any merit is to be able to touch what really is and live it," said Wu. "And if you can do that, it's so profound that you'll have no concern for specialness anyway.

"The strongest man thinks he's special, but weakens and dies. The most beautiful woman thinks she's special, but eventually wrinkles and dies. Neither one will find what really is because of their specialness. They have no reason to look any further. The person who discovers what really is may die, but what they discover neither wrinkles nor weakens, nor does it decay by the trail."

Francisco spoke. "When you discover what really is, it doesn't matter if you're larger than something or infinitely smaller. You're simply in a relationship, no matter the scale of it, no matter the sheer abundance of things living and dying, all the way from insects to the stars."

They sat quietly for a few minutes until Wu spoke again.

"People are overwhelmed by dying and infinity and they create ten-thousand ways to be special in the face of it all, ten-thousand ways to hide this fear of the living and the dying and the rotting under the countless stars and infinite space," Wu said. "They become priests and kings and bankers and salesmen, create religions, ideologies and philosophies, all in order to be special and fight back the fear. Entire groups of people proclaim their uniqueness before God. Poets and artists think they're special. Priests whip themselves to be special. People assume Sanskrit names, worship new gods and goddesses, while others celebrate remaining ignorant like their parents, all in order to still be special. Some wear special clothing. This specialness helps them create excuses for the way they live and what they do to others."

"It seems you only want us to care about you and your concerns," Francisco said. "Do you want us to be less generous to other living things so it can make you feel better?

"You've got to get off this desire to be special and face up to what lies beneath death and infinity. You've made yourself special by holding on to your pain like nobody else has ever felt the same way, but this desire has to end. It will slowly kill you and it's a long terrible dying that lasts your entire lifetime and beyond. You have to get past your fear and special-ness and at least die with dignity."

"That's strange coming from you guys. You don't die."

"Oh, but we will die, and probably sooner than later," Wu replied.

Wu's statement ripped JR open. Despite his anger and frustration he couldn't imagine a life without the old men. He just assumed the old men would continue to be around forever and the idea of them dying was too much to bear. JR had no desire to go back to his old life with no one to talk to, no one to offer guidance or solace. The emptiness of it threatened to engulf him.

Wu took JR's hand and led him to a boulder where he could sit.

"The immensity of the Great Mind is overwhelm-ing and it's far too much for most minds to approach directly. The Great Mind is an inconceivable flow of vastness and energy inside and outside of time and space. The way you can approach it, though, is through your personal god. Your god walks at your side and is your portal to the Great Mind. The world you live in is determined by the god you choose or by the god that was chosen for you when you were too young to choose. When you wake up and assume your fully human life, you can remake your choice of god by imagining a new portal.

"Most gods are bitter, judgmental, and angry, and they subject you to their world. Even people who claim a loving god are, in reality, living at the effect of an angry god that filters their vision of the infinite.

"In a perfect world you would have been special to your parents and they would have been your first gods, then they'd step aside in favor of the gods of the natural world, and they in turn would step aside in favor of a God that unites it all. At the moment you could bear the vision, even God would have to step aside in favor of the full immensity of what really is."

JR tried to absorb what Wu was saying and at the same time tried desperately to keep the thought of the old men's death from his mind.

"You aren't a child anymore and we can't go back and treat you like one. That time is past. You have to forgive your parents for not being enough, forgive the gods for not being enough – even forgive the God you have for not being enough. You have to do all that in order to encounter this immensity of Is-ness and complete your task. It's not a child's task, especially a child who holds onto his wounds in order to create a cocoon of illusion."

Francisco moved next to JR.

"You mean a great deal to us, Maria means a great deal to us, your child means a great deal to us, this world means a great deal to us."

The two men rose and left, leaving JR alone.

After a half hour Francisco and Wu returned. Each of them found a nearby place to sit and faced JR.

Francisco spoke.

"You should know more about Coyote and how he has to carry a terrible burden for the sake of us humans. Maybe then you'll have more compassion for this poor coyote woman here that died trying to bring life to the world. People think Coyote is some sort of evil trickster, but he simply represents the part of our human minds that deceives itself so it can be special, and Coyote gets blamed for it. Truth is, Coyote can only deceive you if you aren't paying attention. So, Coyote is useful. If you pay attention, Coyote is simply a good friend and a reminder. If Coyote pisses you off and steals your money, you need to go deeper, figure out how you're really screwing with yourself."

Francisco chuckled, then continued.

"I'll tell you a story you didn't know about Coyote. He's pretty clever, and that's always his problem. He's everywhere, and he exists in every time you can imagine, though he knows how to disguise himself pretty well. You have to pay attention because you never know when he's going to show up and plot to take your wallet, your wife, or your good name. Some years ago he decided his life would be a whole lot easier if all the easy marks of the world would just up and announce themselves as ripe for the picking since he was more special than them anyway. He wouldn't have to work so hard and he's always looking for the easy way out. He thought about the situation for quite a while, until in a flash of sheer inspiration he came up with an answer. He up and created the smiley face. Now all he had to do was look for the bumper stickers or lapel pins or the cute little face that people draw by their names. Coyote's life was a whole lot easier after that and the pickings were easy. He got a real kick out of that."

Francisco paused.

"You never put one of those stickers on your bumper, did you JR, to mark yourself as special?"

Wu and Francisco laughed so hard they nearly fell off their rocks.

Dusk was approaching so Francisco and Wu rose from their seats and beckoned JR toward the trail. A few minutes after they left, the male coyote emerged from the brush higher up the mountain and approached its mate by the creek. He sniffed at her body and the body of their pup that protruded from her. When he knew for sure they were dead he threw his head back in a great wail.

From where he stood on the other side of the river, JR heard the plaintive, mournful cry to the sky. It pierced him.

Elements of Being iv

The Great Mind winds through the ten-thousand things and knows neither mercy nor greed. We whisper in its ear, "Here is what the ten-thousand things are like." What fate do we choose for existence with our praise and our complaints? Choose your experience and choose your words. Everything matters. Matter depends on you and existence requires you.

Wu Jiyan

PARADISE RIDGE
Summer 2009

The trail rose in switchbacks through the stands of giant sequoia and on up the mountain. JR stopped to catch his breath, but the old men seemed to hardly notice the steep climb. While he paused for a few minutes, JR looked around at the forest of big trees. His mind was caught by the cinnamon color of the massive trunks that seemed to connect earth and sky. JR had visited groves of sequoias by the roadway before, but he'd never hiked through an expanse of them and studied them closely. Wu approached JR, opened his hand and extended it in front of JR's face. At first JR didn't see anything, but then noticed a tiny seed less than an eighth of an inch by a fourth of an inch with tiny wings protruding from it.

"This is where the tree starts, this is where it all starts," Wu said, as he gestured around at the grove with his hand and the seed.

"Where do you start?"

The old men turned back to the trail and continued the steep ascent while JR followed. After they'd gained about two thousand feet of elevation, the three men emerged on an exposed ridge that extended from east to west. Below them the canyon of the Kaweah River extended toward the backcountry.

They turned west on the ridge and made their way across a rocky saddle. Ahead of them granite towers stood at the end of the ridge and marked the edge of the canyon.

The vista of the distant granite peaks pulled forth memories in Wu's mind of his first journey among the sequoias and his first views down into the gorge of the Middle Fork of the Kaweah River. The granite and snow-covered backcountry at the head of the canyon loomed out into his mind. He'd gone with Wu to visit Hale Tharp, the rancher who spent his summers living in a hollow sequoia log while his cattle grazed in the adjacent meadow. The old men sometimes worked for Tharp on his ranch below Three Rivers where Horse Creek flowed into the Kaweah.

Tharp had climbed Moro Rock and managed to set up a system of ropes that other people like his daughter could follow. He'd finally persuaded the old men to climb to the top to take in the expansive vision of the peaks. The climb reminded Wu of the narrow ledges and rope ascents that hermits back in China negotiated to get to and from their caves and small mountain huts. Any doubt he might have about being in the right place was erased when he stood on top of the rock. This was indeed the world

Dizang had meant for him. As if to punctuate the sense of rightness, Wu selected a piece of manzanita for a walking stick on the trip back down the mountain and began to carve Dizang's face into the small burl at the top.

When he surveyed the immensity of the backcountry from the top of Moro Rock, Wu realized it wasn't a place for permanent retreat or habitation. He could only pass through the landscape, befriend it, and learn from it as much as he could, but he couldn't claim it with a permanent dwelling in the high granite. The peaks existed for relationship, not domination. The glacial polish on the peaks on the eastern horizon caught the sun and flashed with an intensity that seemed to illuminate his mind. The old men stayed on the rock until the sun began to set and cast rose hues on the mountainsides.

Across the canyon from Moro Rock stood the stone towers of Castle Rock. That was where Wu now stood. He'd been here many times before with Francisco in retreats from the lower elevations. When he hiked up through the forest of giant sequoias, he was always struck with amazement that some of the trees he was looking at were alive before the First Emperor. It certainly helped him keep a humble perspective on his own 200 years of immortality. He appreciated the lessons of the great trees, and when he looked across the canyon he meditated on the scale of geologic time. It was all part of eating the universe and digesting all it could teach him.

JR and the old men made their way to a position on one of the towers where they could survey the view. Francisco and Wu explained to JR that the ridge they were on was called Paradise Ridge and that nearby was the beginning of Paradise Creek, the same creek that entered the Kaweah near where they'd pulled him from the water. An old trail led from the Paradise Creek bridge up the mountain to the towers of Castle Rock, but large portions of it had disappeared beneath dense thickets of poison oak. The old men preferred the indirect route through the sequoias and their labyrinth of age and grace.

"You know," said Wu. "We're not perfect... especially him."

He pointed toward Francisco and laughed.

"We don't even know why we're still here on this planet, except we love the place."

Francisco mumbled a few unintelligible words and walked away.

JR thought of all he'd experienced in life.

"I know how you'd love these mountains, but how do you love the rest of the world? How can you love all the crappy, screwed-up people and all the violence?"

"You were pretty screwed-up yourself. What were we supposed to do with you, let you drown in the river as punishment? We don't know where this is all going to end up ourselves, but if we judge it and rant against it, things will only be worse. Our minds would get dominated by, and taken over by, all the minds we opposed.

"We may be here to help free people from hell, but we can't oppose hell."

"How do you do that?" asked JR. "You have to oppose all that's bad, oppose everybody who's destroying the world."

Wu studied JR for a moment.

"A Japanese poet once wrote:
Where there are humans,
You'll find flies,
And Buddhas.

"It's not up to us to judge who's a buddha, who's a human, and who's a fly. Sometimes there are flies who are almost buddhas. It wastes our valuable energy to judge it all. Anything changed by opposition hasn't really changed."

Just as Wu finished talking, Francisco returned from relieving himself behind a rock.

"Are you talking that Buddha crap again? He makes it too complicated with that Buddha talk. The Great Mind has us here to complete a task, and if you can do the task, you become what a human being is supposed to be. That's what he calls a Buddha, but I call it a lot of extra words."

Wu scowled at Francisco.

"Ah, the bear returns from shitting in the woods."

Francisco and Wu glared at each other, then laughed uproariously. Francisco took a seat near JR.

"Look out over these mountains and rivers and the backcountry," said Wu. "They have no choice in their formation. All the plants and all the animals that exist here in the mountains have no choice in their formation. You have a choice in your formation, but you've never used it until recently."

"I've made lots of choices, most of them bad."

"You probably never made a real choice in your life until you met us," Francisco said. "You were always reacting to your anger or your dick or your desire for something else. You were always doing what you were impelled to do and thought you were free."

"How is doing what I want to do not being free?"

Francisco exploded into laughter again.

"We pulled you out of the river one gulp from being a corpse. How's that for doing what you want to do? You'll head off on the worst of all possible courses simply because someone tells you not to."

"But that's human nature, that's the way I am and who I am."

Wu joined Francisco in the laughter as Francisco continued.

"You have absolutely no idea who you are, or what it means to really be human, except for what you experience with us and maybe some with Maria. You've just been a human shaped animal with delusions about freedom and choice. You knew all your shit wasn't working or you wouldn't have called us into existence."

"Why me? Why are you here to help me rather than helping someone else? You told me I wasn't special."

"You make us laugh sometimes," said Wu. "You say 'why me?' when you're beset by problems and you say 'why me?' when you're faced with freedom. You have to just accept the gift and the situation and be grateful. It's all very mysterious, and there are no formulas. Enjoy the mystery, immerse yourself in it."

"If that's true, then why am I here, why am I alive?"

"The easiest answer is simply to say 'because you are,' but there are things to do. All you have to do is to stay awake and you'll find the answers you need, but everyone goes to sleep right away and gets pissed if you try to wake them up. All the quests for money and power are attempts to stay asleep. If you wake up, you realize that you carry the possibilities of the universe, and consciously carrying the possibilities of the universe is freedom."

"What happens if I stay awake?"

"If you really stay awake you learn how to choose, and when you cross the river to the other side, you can choose what's next. Real choice appears as the most frightening thing in the world to someone who's asleep. They'll kill, maim, and torture to remain asleep. They'll bury themselves beneath their illusions and ideologies and things and quests for power in order to hide and sleep."

Francisco swept his arm out over the canyon and the backcountry.

"It's hard to imagine that someone could look out into this vista and not be changed, not wake up. Truth is, the people who refuse to wake up are afraid of life, pissed off at life and want to punish it. They'd punish all this if they could. They punish anyone who is awake or close to being awake. Being asleep means being at the mercy of hell. Those who are asleep have created a world where there's a great profit to be made from punishing life and living in hell. It's the illusion we live in."

Francisco again gestured toward the backcountry.

"Try as we humans might with our best efforts, none of this world can really be saved unless we choose to wake up from hell."

"It's a next to impossible job to bring wakefulness to the world," said Wu, "but not totally impossible.

However, it's the only real job there is. The other things you do in life are merely to support it. Imagine a world where people's daily work of survival was also their real work of being awake in the world."

"Being awake in partnership with the Great Mind is our true fate beneath the stars" said Francisco, "and it frees us."

"What's my true fate?" said JR. "I'm not much of anyone, just a cowboy."

"Be an awakened cowboy," said Francisco, "and see where it leads you and who you meet. You can't go out to save anyone. If someone asks for your help in being free, then you give it. Sometimes they even float by in the river."

"It doesn't sound like enough," said JR.

"It's all there is," said Wu. "It's all we can do. Everything else is shuffling the furniture."

STALKING
December 2009

Francisco situated himself behind a rock on a small hill a short distance from the cave mouth where he could watch the demon without being seen. After years of searching, he'd finally stalked the demon to its lair. He was surrounded by oak trees and manzanita in an area that had burned years ago. Around him life was reclaiming the landscape. Suddenly the demon appeared at the cave entrance and made its way out into an open area where Francisco could see it. It still looked like Padre Serra and still carried the glass-tailed scourge. The demon's eyes scoured the landscape and for a moment seemed to light on the spot where Francisco was hiding.

Francisco didn't quite know what he'd do if the demon spotted him. They'd wrestled before, but there was never a winner – in fact the immediate landscape had been burned and destroyed by one of their matches in the past. The devastation to the world was never worth the direct confrontation.

As Francisco watched the demon, he remembered traveling to the mission at Carmel on a trading and supply trip when he was a boy. He was taken through the mission church where Padre Serra was buried beneath the floor, and when no one was looking, he'd spat on the padre's grave with a vengeance. Until he escaped, it was the only act of defiance he'd allowed himself, and it was the moment the demon's mask was forged from his anger.

Francisco's thoughts and memories ran through his mind in a fraction of a second. When he regained his focus, he discovered Padre Serra staring at him from the other side of the rock. The padre flicked the scourge like a mountain lion flicking its tail before its prey. The good father raised the whips and leaped toward Francisco, the glass shards flashing in the light.

Francisco woke with a start and found the room filling with morning light that danced off a mirror on the wall. He recoiled in defense as a shadow fell across his body, but it was Wu standing over him with a concerned look on his face, and with the staff in his hand. Francisco sat up on the edge of the bed and tried to gain his bearings as the padre's face hung before his mind's eye. He could feel the time was near. Wu leaned on his staff for a moment before he walked out of the room and out of the cabin. He knew it would soon be time to free Francisco from his last bit of hell.

CAVE
December 2009

JR woke to a drizzling rain outside the cave entrance. The days were shorter as the planet approached the winter solstice.

The old men had told him it was time to be free.

"It's time to confront your demon," Francisco said, "the one that patrols the entrance to the hole in your being.

"In the old days we would have given you a tea of datura, but it's not a very good idea for you. You're always too close to the edge and the tea would only make you crazy."

"The man who knew how to pick and prepare the tea died long ago," Wu said, "soon after I went through the journey. We'd be fools to proceed to without the old knowledge. Besides, your mind doesn't need it. You're close, very close."

The cave looked like an ancient den for a bear. The narrow opening between boulders quickly widened and then turned in toward the mountain behind one of the boulders so little direct light entered. With the sun low on the southern horizon and the cave on a north-facing slope, only a dim diffuse light illuminated the interior during the day. The cave was near where Francisco pulled him from the river a lifetime ago.

JR didn't know what to do. He wasn't good at just sitting around. He had always been propelled by a nervous energy that seemed beyond his power to manage. He rolled out his sleeping bag in the back of the cave. He was told not to eat, but he'd brought a water bottle. Nearby a small creek was flowing if he needed more water and down the hill he could hear the low roaring sound of a set of rapids on the Kaweah.

The first day was hard. He couldn't stand fully upright in the cave and so he paced nervously in front of the entrance to relieve the tedium. He was supposed to stay in the cave as much as possible but he knew he couldn't do it. The words of an old hymn from childhood circled through his mind.

Rock of Ages,
Cleft for me,
Let me hide myself in thee.

He reflected on the things that had transpired since he'd been pulled from the river and he thought about the old men. They didn't belittle him, but they didn't tell him how good he was either. They matter-of-factly accepted him like it was the way things should be. Maybe it really was the way things should be.

There were a lot of people who'd made fewer mistakes than he had and they'd done more and been more, and yet these crazy old men took him under wing. There was no logic to it at all and he still struggled to accept the reality of the situation.

JR remembered the dream about flying up through the storm and felt a surge of strength and purpose.

It began to rain, forcing him to stay inside the cave. He thought of Maria and Sophia. Sophia was now close to two years old and he needed to make decisions. He knew he wanted to be with his family, but he didn't know how he could provide for them. He was frightened of this mysterious world he was walking through with the old men, a fundamental world of such energy, grace, and color that it overwhelmed him. The everyday world he experienced in the past was one of such small-minded pettiness and violence that he was afraid when he tried to imagine living in this new world, the world-beneath-the-world. He would be left defenseless, vulnerable, and subject to death at any moment.

He didn't know how he'd manage in the everyday world if he gave himself completely to the new reality. It wasn't just a matter of his own survival. Now Maria and Sophia were coming to depend on his presence and his ability to survive. He was just a cowboy and he depended on being in the outdoors away from the madness that people had created and he didn't know what else he could do with himself. He didn't think cowboying would be enough anymore, but for the moment he had no other options.

JR also knew his old way of struggling with the everyday world wouldn't work anymore. If he forged ahead into the new world it seemed as if he'd die, but if he tried to go back to what he had been, he'd die for sure.

He thought back to November when he went down to the flatland to be with Maria and Sophia. They'd seen some kind of festival happening by the oak forest between two of the creeks and decided to walk through it. In the middle of a field he saw a painter – some peach farmer – wearing a broad hat and it seemed as if the colors were coming out of the man's fingers. JR watched the peach farmer paint and felt an arousal – the old feeling of being overtaken by colors and shapes – and the feeling ran through his body from his belly and balls in all directions like a slow electric fire. When they returned to Maria's, they made love. She was wearing the dark green earrings he'd given her and the green against her skin and hair carried him away to the other world.

The cave walls began to change around him. The walls were now lit by flickering torches and covered by paintings of strange animals across the undulating stone. Lions and bison and rhinoceros, bears and deer. Without understanding why, JR picked up a piece of charcoal and began drawing the outlines of a bear on the wall nearest him. He labored for hours and while he worked he heard human voices – sometimes chanting, sometimes singing – in an unknown language. He also felt eyes watching his movements. When the last strokes were added, the bear suddenly came to life and reached out toward him from the stone.

It roared.

JR woke up slumped against the cave wall. He reached out and touched the rock to gain his bearings and remember where he was. It was the cave wall above the Kaweah and it was dark again. He was alone except for whatever rodents inhabited the place. JR had no idea what time it was, though he still had the sense of being watched. It seemed like someone was writing down his story and trying to decide where it might go, trying to choose among countless possibilities. JR concentrated his thoughts and attempted to communicate a vision of life for him and his family.

He spread himself out in his sleeping bag to wait for the dim glow of morning light. When he closed his eyes he saw himself hurtling over a hill in a sportscar in a wild rush of frantic speed. He felt invincible, alive, immortal. Directly in front of him a car turned left.

JR opened his eyes. It seemed to be morning as best he could tell and the sound of the river had wakened him. The noise of the tumbling whitewater increased until it seemed he would go deaf. After a few minutes the sound died away. That was how the everyday world was to him at times, reaching such a crescendo of volume that he didn't know how to cope with the noise. And it was noise. No melody, certainly no harmony, and no words that he could understand. In those moments the world made such little sense that he could only run or drink.

When he was painting on the cave wall, JR felt connected. He was connected to the people who'd made the other paintings and he was connected to the animals in the paintings and to the walls of the cave itself. The walls had undulated around him in live organic shapes and around his feet were scattered the bones of animals that once used the place for shelter. He felt like he was inside a live creature with a mind of its own. In everyday life, everything felt separated and isolated, except for his new family and the old men, and he felt like a creature that had been hacked into pieces, and though he was still alive, none of the pieces were connected, could no longer move in concert, could no longer walk, run, sing, or paint. His bones were scattered. That existence now seemed a living death and he knew he couldn't go back. He grasped at a future.

The rain stopped so JR decided to step outside the cave to walk around and relieve himself. He stayed outside as long as he could until the rain began again.

He tried to alternate sitting in one place with lying down on his sleeping bag. Occasionally he'd go outside again when his body would no longer be still and the rain wasn't too heavy. There was no real ventilation for a fire to dry him out, so he had to avoid getting very wet.

He reached a point where he felt like he was going to explode. At the moment he wanted to rip the top of his head off and go running out into the storm, the cave mouth began to move. It opened and closed from top to bottom, then began to widen and sprout enormous triangular teeth with serrated edges. Behind him at the back of the cave, JR heard the sudden roar of a bear. The roar startled him and the force of the sound made him want to run. Freedom appeared through gaps in the interlocking teeth, but none of the openings was large enough for him to squeeze through. He stared at the openings until the pent up energy in his mind and body exploded and he threw himself at the teeth anyway. Each time he tried to squeeze through the gaps, his body grated against the serrated edges. His skin ripped.

JR fell back into exhaustion, his body stiffened with pain and covered with blood. He closed his eyes. When he opened them, he discovered he was tied to a tree, struggling to get free. The pain wracked his body and he fought back the urge to scream. Images of his mother and father back in Missouri swam through his mind, along with memories of beatings, abuse, and the empty longing for something more in life. He felt isolated and alone with a pain far greater than the pain of his bloody body.

JR focused his eyes on a man standing in front of him. The man raised his knife and began to cut away JR's skin. The man stopped for a moment, thrust his face toward JR's face, and looked deeply into his eyes. JR wanted to spit or laugh in the man's face to show contempt for the pain, but stopped in horror.

The face belonged to Francisco.

JR screamed, and the scream echoed the pain of lifetimes. He screamed his sense of betrayal and rage, and the rage propelled him screaming out the cave opening and into the night and the pouring rain. Somewhere up the mountain a single male coyote wailed in response.

He ran as fast he could manage through the rocks and brush and back to his truck, then aimed it downhill toward civilization.

He felt hollow, alone, and afraid.

The Story shifted to find a new path among the possibilities.

THE WATCHERS
December 2009

Francisco and Wu watched JR's cave from a ridge further up the mountain where there was an overhanging ledge to help keep out the rain. They took turns waiting and watching. They were concerned about JR's state of mind and his ability to deal with the task they'd put before him. Maybe it was too soon, but they didn't know how much longer they'd be around. They left JR at the cave and, when they were out of sight, headed up the mountain on a game trail.

During the third night, Francisco had another dream of Padre Serra. Francisco was at the demon's lair again, the entrance layered with bones, and was watching it from a distance. The padre moved out of the cave over the bones and into Francisco's field of view. The moment the padre looked over in Francisco's direction, a piercing scream roused him from his dream and from his sleep. From down mountain came more screams and the sounds of a body hurtling through brush and over loose rocks.

Francisco knew he'd failed and with that realization he felt the scourge bite deeply into his back.

HELL
December 2009

JR slowly opened his eyes. He could smell strange
odors and make out odd shapes around him. He was
in a strange room, one he'd never been in before and
he was lying in bed with someone. He slowly looked
to his left where a woman was lying across his arm. It
wasn't Maria, but she wasn't exactly a stranger. It was
the young woman he'd seen down at the Mountain
House with her boyfriend a long time ago, the one
he thought was too high maintenance, the one he'd
seen right before he fell into the river. Her hair was
askew like she'd just been fucked and the air smelled
of some cheap perfume mixed with cigarette smoke.
He began to remember the last few days and he felt
dirty. He wanted to chew his arm off to get away like
a coyote in a trap.

He'd come home from the cave and started drinking. He felt angry and betrayed, and the pain was more
than he could bear. He'd gone to the bar, had a lot
more to drink, and run into Miss High Maintenance.
She'd just split with her boyfriend and she was the one
who put all the moves on, but he fell into it.

He was too drunk to care much about anything and let her drive him to her house. His body rebelled though, like it knew better, and it was like trying to push rope, so he gave up and fell asleep. He looked her over again and, mercifully, she rolled off his arm and sat up, poked at her hair, then pulled on a bra and some thong panties.

"Gotta piss."

She staggered away, pulling the stained thong strap into her butt crack.

JR lay back for a minute and realized with a start that he could feel her existence. He felt her turmoil and pain and it pressed on him until he felt suffocated by the weight. He was glad they weren't able to have sex. He knew if they had, he'd have become even more entangled with her reality and it would've near destroyed him. As it was, he was in bad shape.

When she came out of the bathroom, JR started pulling on his clothes and looking for his boots. She looked at him and laughed.

"Boy, big guy like you, I thought it'd be better than that."

She held up a limp little finger and wiggled it.

JR didn't say a word, just pulled on his boots and walked out the door. He'd felt the anger rise in him at the comment and the gesture, but he was tired of his anger, tired of being taken over and jerked around, tired of waking up in the places his anger led him. He headed out to the road and began walking back to the bar where he'd left his truck

When he got home he stripped off all his clothes and sat in the middle of the floor naked. The enormity of the situation bore down upon him and pinned him to the floor. He was right back where he used to be, only worse, because now he knew better. He began to cry. He wanted the tears to make it all go away, but they didn't. They simply highlighted his pain. He hadn't really made a choice to do all the things he did the past few days. The anger just took over and threw him hurtling down the mountain to this pile of shit wreckage.

JR pulled himself into the shower and began trying to scrub the anger away. He ritually scrubbed himself from one end to the other, attacking the anger, the cheap perfume smell, and the cigarette smoke. His attack gradually softened until he finally moved slowly with regret and remorse. More memories slipped into his mind. There were some old men, but he couldn't even remember their names.

After he got out of the shower, he wiped the steam off the mirror and looked at his face. He studied his beard, then opened a drawer and pulled out scissors and a razor. He wasn't leaving any place for his fear and anger to lurk. He cut away the hair. It was the least he could do in contrition.

JR suddenly remembered something one of the old men said. "People are always making excuses for their anger and making a god of it because the anger is what makes people feel large and real."

JR knew he couldn't bear up under the anger any longer or he would for sure kill himself like his daddy had. He had to get off the goddamned wheel. He knew the old men were the key, but not only couldn't he remember their names, he couldn't even remember where they lived.

JR put some water on for tea. He didn't know why he was doing it or why he even had tea in his house. When the tea was ready he went outside to look out at the mountains. He wanted to go jump in the creek, but the weather was cold and gray. While he sipped the tea, memories of Maria and Sophia took over his mind and he found the memories both a blessing and a curse. He couldn't believe he'd experienced such joy with the two of them, but the realization of what he'd done, of what his anger had done, was enough to throw him back into despair. Somehow his only hope lay with them. He was overcome by his sorrow and loss, and overcome by the sorrow of the world around him.

JR wept.

He tried to imagine redemption.

Elements of Being v

Scientists and priests have difficulty seeing what is real, bound by their conceptions and laws. A crow cries out in flight, a coyote howls, and that is enough for understanding. The ten-thousand things are mundane, matter-of-fact, yet breath-takingly supernatural. Look up from your feeding bowl, see the mystery, and get to your work. Use the tools at hand to show the world its true nature. Life is meant to be, mind is meant to be – carry this fire of mind, free those in hell.

Wu Jiyan

OFF THE WHEEL
December 2009

She was pregnant again. Maria was positive she'd taken care of birth control, but even with that she knew exactly when the conception occurred. She knew it in the moment. It was after the three of them walked through the festival out between the creeks and seen the painter at his easel. When they returned home JR exploded in her with a passionate intensity that overwhelmed her with colors and forms and mountains and rivers. She could feel life beginning to kindle in her, but she didn't know how JR would take the news. She was sure he loved both her and Sophia, but she still had no idea where the relationship would lead. He managed to surprise her often and express a sincerity of which she never thought him capable.

After he left for the mountains with Wu and Francisco five or six days ago, Maria had impulsively bought JR a gift to lead into the discussion about their new child. She kept the gift in her purse waiting for him to come back, but he hadn't been in touch and she was worried. Being a father was now serious business to him.

She was getting dressed to go to work when she heard a knock at the door. She found him standing in the doorway, looking dazed, and she had to do a double take when she saw his shaved face with its pained expression unfiltered by the beard.

"I can't remember."

Maria was alarmed. She brought him into the house and sat him down. She knew the situation would take far more time to solve than she had available, so she called in sick and then canceled daycare for Sophia. When she turned back to JR, he was staring vacantly into space.

"Take me to the old guys, don't remember their names, don't remember how to get there."

Maria changed her clothes and quickly dressed Sophia. She knew her little car wouldn't be any good for the old dirt road into Francisco and Wu's place. She walked over to JR.

"Give me your keys,"

She picked up Sophia and led JR to the passenger side of the truck. Once he was inside she handed Sophia to him and then climbed behind the wheel, fired up the engine, and pointed the truck in the direction of the mountains. She wanted to drive as fast as she could, but around her the sky was dense with winter tule fog. When she approached intersections she had to hang her head out the window to listen for the muffled sounds of traffic that might come from either side. She knew she'd probably rise out of the fog somewhere below Three Rivers, but until then it was going to take a long time. JR stared vacantly out the window and made no effort to talk as the fog slid by and hid any scenery that might possibly help pull him from his pit. Occasionally Sophia attempted to use her few words to get her father's attention, but JR would smile for a moment, then lapse back into painful emptiness.

Maria didn't have a clue what was going on with JR, but she had to help him in any way she could, if only for the sake of her daughter. She knew she couldn't save him, but at least she could take him to the old men, and, after that, she'd see where things stood. In the meantime she had to fight her own fear, not only the fear that she might lose what she had with JR, but also the fear that she was being dragged across a line into another world, a world that would distort what she held to be real.

What had happened, what had he done?

CRYING, DANCING
December 2009

After JR hurtled down the mountain and took the truck, Wu and Francisco made their way back to Hospital Rock, where it started to rain again. They took shelter under the rock where the Potwisha used to hold their ceremonies. They could have waited on the other side of the road in a restroom or under an arbor, but the rock with the old painting was a better place. After a few hours a car stopped – someone returning from the first heavy snows of the year – and they were able to get a ride. At Mineral King Road they started walking up the narrow, twisting pavement until eventually someone gave them another ride.

Francisco couldn't seem to shake the priest from his consciousness. Wu watched Francisco closely, but restrained himself from using the staff. As painful as it was for the old Yokuts to endure the padre's visits, they both knew the time wasn't quite right. Finally, on the night before the winter solstice, they both had the same dream. They were watching Padre Serra's lair together when, with a roar, a giant grizzly chased the priest out of the cave. The priest turned and raised his scourge as the bear advanced, but the bear slashed out with its five-inch long claws, hooked the scourge and pulled it away. The priest cowered in fear. Wu stepped out from hiding, raised his staff and tapped the old priest's head in a gesture of absolution and benediction. When the carved head touched the priest's tonsure, the padre slowly transformed into the figure of Dizang. The bodhisattva looked in the direction of Francisco, Wu, and the bear, raised his palms together and bowed, then dissolved from sight.

When they woke, Wu and Francisco went about their personal morning rituals. They chose to eat nothing as they waited for the day – the shortest day, the darkest day – to reach its conclusion. Wu finally tapped Francisco on the forehead with Dizang's staff and chanted his prayers for the freeing of all beings from hell.

Soon the old men heard the truck coming up the road and waited for the sound of the engine to stop. They walked out of the cabin in silence and waited.

Maria and Sophia approached Francisco and Wu with JR shuffling alongside. When JR approached Francisco, he simply said, "I'm sorry," and began weeping.

Francisco put his arms around JR and whispered in JR's ear, "I'm sorry, too, my son."

There was a lot more that JR wanted to convey and pour out of his being, but it was too complex for words. The two words had to tell it all. When he said them and heard Francisco's reply he began to remember everything – everything that had been done to him, everything he had done to others. He remembered the deal he made by the river long ago and felt the deep immeasurable regret that comes with awareness. He remembered all his many parents and all their parents and knew there was no one he could blame. All he could do was wake up from the inheritance of this pain-ridden trance and be different, be alive.

Francisco pressed his forehead to JR's. JR's reality shifted and he found himself in front of a group of kneeling men in robes at the top of a hill. It was the middle of the night and several torches were held aloft to light the ceremony. He was flanked on either side by Wu and Francisco.

One of the kneeling men at the front of the group called out, "Shall we call him a Buddha?"

"No," Wu replied. "He must choose his own name."

JR heard a droning chant come from the kneeling men, then found he was back at the cabin, standing in front of Francisco. Francisco kissed him on the forehead and whispered in his ear.

"No name is fine…so is JR. Don't let the Buddha shit go to your head and make you too special."

After a pause, JR kissed Francisco back. They put their foreheads together once again and began to dance the slow shuffling grieving dance while Francisco chanted in Yokuts.

JR stopped for a moment to go pick up Sophia and to draw Maria into the dance. Wu chanted his prayers for the freeing of all beings from hell, and then joined everyone in the shuffling, crying circle, the child held in the middle of it all, the grief for all beings cleansing the air and their minds.

After awhile they stopped and went inside the cabin, where Wu prepared tea. Francisco looked at Maria for a moment.

"When is your son going to come and be with us?"

Surprised, Maria replied, "Sometime in August." She looked anxiously toward JR .

WORST FEARS
December 2009

Maria didn't know what to make of the things she'd witnessed up at the old men's cabin, but she knew something had changed for JR. In her mad rush to get him to the cabin she wasn't able to dwell on what it was that made him so like a zombie and had cut him so deeply. It had been days since she'd returned and now her mind was beginning to knot up around the question. Maria's instinct and her carefully honed fear both told her there was another woman involved.

The thought of another woman scared the hell out of her. She remembered how it was when her dad left for another woman. He hadn't even said good-bye or tried to explain himself. He just left a note saying he'd been unhappy for a long time and then he moved in with the woman. Maria didn't even think the woman was that pretty, certainly not enough to lure a man away from his family. The only thing Maria saw that was different was the other woman didn't have any kids, and the fact hurt Maria deeply. In her heart Maria knew her father left because of her and her sister. They were chains to him. Sometimes she wondered what she could have done differently so he would have stayed, but mostly she knew it was simply her existence that had driven him away.

Maria hadn't spoken to JR since Francisco divined the truth about her pregnancy up at the cabin. She'd driven home that night because JR was in a euphoric trance on their way back down the mountain. When they approached the valley floor the fog engulfed them again and it took all her attention to navigate the road. At home they put Sophia to bed, then fell into bed themselves. She dragged herself out of bed the next day for work, and when she came home JR was gone.

A hole had been created in her mind where all her fears could enter. If there was another woman, it would be the end. There was no way she'd put her children through the torture of what she experienced when she was young, and she was certainly not willing to relive her own feelings of not being enough and of feeling wrong for simply existing.

Besides that, the whole notion of crossing over into JR's world like Francisco once told her was confusing and frightening. It had a lot to do with the kids, but it also had a lot to do with what a life as a couple, as a family, should look like. It seemed that life in the mountains was a necessity for JR and she didn't know how to work around the fact. She had her desires and comforts. No matter what the old men told her about giving up illusion, she had no ongoing experience of what that was like. When they all danced around Sophia, Maria felt a warmth and openness, an openness to something else, but the effects of the dance were being pushed away by her fear.

When JR finally returned, the fear and the questions welled up in her as he walked into the living room. She blurted out what was on her mind.

"What was it, what did you do?"

JR half-expected the question, but he also hoped it would never come up. He'd paid dearly for his anger during his lifetime and he'd nearly lost everything this last go around. If she hadn't asked the question there was a good chance he would never have said anything. He simply didn't want to lose his family. He wasn't just hoping things would be different for him and his anger – he knew it was different. He'd felt the hard knot at his core dissolve to nothingness when he embraced and kissed Francisco, and the ceremony in front of the kneeling men altered his sense of who he was. It felt like lifetimes of convoluted and distorted living had been suddenly set straight.

JR told her the story without evasion. When he told her about the woman, Maria pushed at him wildly, then shoved him out the door as she beat on his chest. Once outside he stood at a short distance from her to say his last words.

"I was wrong, but please don't make me wrong forever. I love you and Sophia too much."

He wanted to kiss her, but knew that to her it might feel like rape, so he turned back toward his truck and left.

Maria watched him leave. She knew she couldn't be everything for JR, but she still wanted to be. Maybe if she'd been able to be his everything, then he'd have had no reason to betray her.

All around her the hopes and dreams she'd built and lived in crashed into the sandy soil of the walnut orchard along the river. She was a pregnant single mother, alone in the dust.

EMPTY
January 2010

JR's mind probed the empty recesses that used to be filled with his anger. It was like when he had a tooth pulled and his tongue kept going back to explore the empty hole over and over, not quite comprehending there was actually nothing there anymore. It wasn't that the anger was completely gone. There were the normal daily tidal movements of irritations and provocations to deal with, but the overwhelming tsunami of lifetimes of rage was gone.

Wu once told him that dealing with irritations and frustrations was like catching flies out of the air with his hand. Catching them out of the air meant he could choose what to do with them without reacting blindly. JR's rage had been like blowing up a house because there were flies in it. Now he understood how he might catch them and release them outside where they belonged. JR also had the sense he might be able to walk through a swarm of flies and not be bothered, that the swarm could simply part before his face.

The emptiness in his mind felt strange. It felt like depression, but it wasn't really depression. The anger had filled so many recesses of his mind that JR had come to believe that the anger was who he was, that it was his identity. He didn't know how to fill the void and it scared him.

JR also felt an acute pain at the loss of his family, a pain he could only observe and do nothing about. He couldn't ignore the pain, neither could he medicate it. He also knew he couldn't chase Maria down and try to make everything okay. He accepted responsibility for what had happened and didn't want to talk his way out of the situation. He didn't want to attempt to convince Maria of anything. He could only hope the strange path of fate that had released him from his hell would also lead Maria to understand things for herself. She had to choose for herself, free of her own fear and free of his begging for forgiveness.

It was strange that he'd been released from his hell only to lose his family in the process. JR loved both Maria and Sophia deeply, and losing them wasn't a choice he would consciously make. He knew though, that in reality, he and his family couldn't have survived any great length of time as long as he was a prisoner. JR had to be grateful to the old men for his freedom while at the same time he mourned the loss of Maria and their children.

JR's only recourse was to do what needed to be done around the ranch and to ride out among the mountains while life began to grow and spread like wildflowers through all the places his anger had once filled with darkness. Colors began to seize him and extinguish fear.

CROSSING THE LINE
January 2010

Maria felt like she was pushing the car up the dirt road toward the old men's cabin. She was driving her own car and it was just too low and too old. It had been weeks since she'd last seen JR, and the weight of his betrayal combined with her desperation was almost too much to bear.

Maria tried to talk to her mom, but her mom didn't have much to offer other than, "That's just the way men are." Though it was tempting to fall into the sentiment for consolation, it did nothing to get to the heart of Maria's pain. She hadn't felt this much pain since her father left. She'd always believed he'd come back if she loved him enough, but he died of a heart attack after a few years and had never come back. With JR gone, Maria was left again with the inadequacy of her loving. The fear and pain had become too much and now she needed some form of relief so she could be a mother to her children.

Maria went to see her grandmother whom she hadn't talked to for quite awhile. Maria quickly sketched in the story of JR and the old men and her predicament. Her grandmother's eyes came alive with the story and she sang to herself.

"You must go to the old men again."

Maria remembered her first time at the cabin. She remembered the fear she'd felt, but she also remembered the calm that followed when the old men touched her. The faces of her ancestors pressed on her memory and even though she felt the weight of the vast sorrow, there was also a strange peace in seeing and acknowledging the sorrow of her people. Maria wondered if the ancestors might now tell her something to relieve the fear and the pain.

"Yes, you must see the old men again," her grandmother said, "for the ancestors, and for your children."

Francisco opened the door of the cabin as Maria's car came to a stop outside. She stepped out of the car and approached the old man. Francisco extended his arms. She was afraid she'd be met with a stern lecture, but instead she fell into his arms.

"I'm your uncle," Francisco said, "many generations removed, but I'm still your uncle. You should know I'd do anything for you."

At Francisco's words, Maria felt herself collapse inward. He took her arm and led her inside the cabin where she could sit at the table. There had always been a strand, an undercurrent, in Maria's family of the men not measuring up, of the sense that, of course they're going to disappoint you. The injustice toward women was woven into the fabric of Maria's life and there was always a sense of women against the hard male world. This old man was claiming to be her uncle and saying he'd do anything for her. The shock to Maria was that she knew it was true. She knew Francisco could be trusted, she knew he would do whatever he could on her behalf.

Maria explained to Francisco what had happened.

"I once told you that you had a choice about whether to cross the line into the world we inhabit, the world JR inhabits, but you're rapidly getting to the place where you'll have no choice either. He had a gaping hole ripped in his life, whereas you have something knocking at your door. Knocking hard, but it's still only knocking. You can choose to answer the door before it gets broken down."

Maria felt impatient and tried to explain again how wronged she felt.

"JR may have wronged you, but in the end he saved me from hell," said Francisco. "If you could only understand the anger and the fury he had to master in order to do that, then you might understand – you might even forgive."

Maria felt herself recoil at the word "forgive."

"Some things are just unforgivable," she said. All her wounds of betrayal lay raw and exposed, and they demanded something to appease their existence.

Francisco looked her in the eye.

"I killed him – not swiftly or mercifully – but slowly and painfully with a great deal of anger. I would have skinned a deer or an antelope with a lot more respect than I gave him. We've both suffered."

Francisco reached out and touched Maria's forehead. She was suddenly looking through his eyes at his hands as they moved a knife around the body of a bearded man tied to a tree. The body was bloody and raw with half its skin pulled away. Maria looked in the bearded man's eyes and felt a taste of the pain he was enduring. Her body winced and writhed at the sudden sensation.

"If you felt all his pain your mind wouldn't be able to survive," Francisco told her. "That pain is what has propelled JR around in his life like a pinball."

When she heard Francisco's words, Maria felt herself pulled back into the room away from the bloody scene, but a memory of the pain remained.

"Two things have saved JR from hell. The first is that we've been given the chance to forgive each other, and the other is that he's chosen to love you and your children.

"The ocean of human suffering is vast and the first task for each of us is to add nothing more to it. If possible, we should do all we can to reduce it by even a cubic inch. JR removed my suffering by giving up his personal pain. Just the two of you together with your children would help reduce suffering in the world by far, far more than a cubic inch.

"It's your choice to make."

The door opened behind her and Maria heard Wu's voice.

"It's time."

"Time for what?" Maria said.

She suddenly felt herself pushed toward a decision she didn't want to make.

"We're leaving," said Wu. "Tell JR to be here in two weeks. You too, if you want to say goodbye."

Maria was confused. Leaving for where? This was their home. She was frightened by the sudden shift in her relationship with the old men. She had to figure things out quickly, because she didn't know what she'd do without Francisco.

GONE
January 2010

Maria caught a ride with JR to the cabin. She wasn't as angry she'd been, but the sense of betrayal remained with her. She could at least ride in the same vehicle with him, though mostly in silence. It was more important for her to see Francisco one last time before the old men left, rather than hold firmly to her anger, so she accepted the offer of a ride. Her old vehicle just wasn't up to traveling this road again.

JR seemed different. He didn't seem as haunted. He seemed deeply sad, but not haunted, and Maria didn't know what to make of the fact that JR never begged for forgiveness. He simply apologized the one time and went back to his life. In some ways it would have been more satisfying to reject him over and over as a continuing punishment, but he didn't give her the pleasure. His refusal to beg and to beat himself in front of her left the emotion of the issue solely with her, and she was tired of keeping up the dynamics of the anger on her own.

Maria still remembered the intensity of her experience of JR's mind as he was being flayed and she wondered if it was possible for anyone to possibly recover from the insanity of it. She wondered what kind of force could possibly heal the raw pain of such trauma. Her experience was a double-edged sword. On the one hand it gave her some sense of compassion, but it also made her hesitant to let their children grow up in the presence of such pain.

JR parked his truck at the cabin and opened his door, then, with an effort at gallantry, opened the door for Maria and their unborn child. They watched as the old men walked from behind the cabin, the mountain lion at their side.

JR once told Maria about seeing the lion, so she wasn't surprised, though it unnerved her. Maria looked around at the cabin and the setting and wondered what would happen to all this if the old men left. A whole way of life was represented by the place and it would soon be gone. She studied the mountains around her and the trees near the cabin – the oaks, the sycamores. She listened to the flow of the creek and could hear the breeze in the trees. She heard a raven in the distance and watched a redtail circle overhead. She felt her ancestors pulling at her.

All this, all this.

It was all so much larger than her fears. Her love for Francisco pulled at her and she felt a deep sorrow that he wouldn't be there to guide her anymore. She didn't know how she'd fill the empty place she never knew she had.

Francisco and Wu embraced JR and Maria, then began a small ritual. The old men each bowed in the four directions and thanked the earth for hosting them as long as it had, then, laughing, they each took a handful of dirt and rubbed it on the other as a memory of the place. They embraced JR and Maria again, then began walking the trail up the mountain with the lion at their side. About 100 yards away, each of the old men bent over and said something in the lion's ear. The lion walked away, paused to look back, then continued walking. Francisco and Wu joined hands, crested a rise in the trail and disappeared.

Maria looked at JR and was overcome. He was the last vestige of this vast experience, the last vestige of the old men. The disappearance of the old men affected her more deeply than she could have imagined. Her love and affection for them began to penetrate deeper than her anger and hurt, and uprooted the pain.

With the pain gone it was clear to her she wanted to live in the world Francisco had shown her, and the only way she knew it could possibly happen was to be with JR.

"Give up the illusion of romance," the old men had said. Love wasn't about the romantic feelings, it was about the relationship with life you cultivate in your time with each other.

Maria remembered her bag in the truck and went to retrieve it. In it was the small gift meant for JR. She'd been carrying the gift for a while, unable to throw it away even though she was angry.

"Here, this is for you, from Sophia and me and…"

She pointed to her belly.

JR opened the gift to find a handful of artist's brushes in a bag. As he stared at the brushes, the colors of the world flooded through him and he remembered the painter in the middle of the oak forest near Maria's house. JR was infused with color, ecstatic with color. Just as he reached to embrace Maria, a sudden cry of anguish came from up the mountain.

JR and Maria ran up the trail where they found Francisco standing in the middle of the path weeping. Wu was nowhere to be found. JR looked down and discovered Wu's staff lying next to a pile of clothes. He carefully pulled the clothes apart only to find a mound of dust inside them.

Francisco sang his mourning song for a few minutes then stopped.

"My friend is gone. How can I live without my friend?

"How will things be real without my friend?"

While Francisco sang and chanted, JR realized he was still carrying the bag and brushes. He handed the brushes to Maria and then carefully scooped the dust into the bag. They both moved to embrace Francisco.

"Something called me back."

After a few minutes, Francisco picked up Wu's staff and turned with Maria and JR back down the trail toward the cabin. After walking a few hundred yards they came upon Jesusito sprawled by the trail holding his knee.

"Thank God, you have found me."

Despite his anguish, Francisco couldn't help but laugh. He helped Jesusito from the ground and motioned JR to help.

"Any new tattoos, my friend? One of these days when you're ready, I'm going to use this stick on you," Francisco said in Spanish. "Maybe even when you're not ready."

Francisco waved the staff in front of the bewildered Jesusito and helped him hobble to the cabin.

WAHAH YAKOW
March 2010

Francisco, JR, and Maria made their way up the steps of the rock and Jesusito waited for them back in the parking lot. JR called it Moro Rock, but Francisco still called it Wahah Yahkow in the old way. Francisco walked with Wu's staff in hand and carried a pouch of Wu's dust. Maria's pregnancy showed visibly, but she would let nothing dissuade her from making the pilgrimage in honor of Wu. She walked slowly and the men were satisfied to move at her pace.

Things had changed. JR was offered a job managing a ranch out the South Fork in Three Rivers. There was a house for them all and JR had bought some canvas and some paints. He'd even contacted the peach farmer about teaching him how to paint. He wanted to express the color of being in this world devoid of his once unbearable weight of remorse. The ranch was also close enough to the cabin that they could go to it whenever they wanted.

In searching through Wu's few belongings, they'd found a handwritten journal in both English and Chinese. He'd called it "Elements of Being."

They had to wait for the snow to melt enough so they could get to the rock and climb the steps again. They wound through the folds and fissures of the rock until they finally reached the top high above the Kaweah River. Toward the backcountry the mountains were still solid fields of glistening snow and ice.

Wu was coming home to the peaks he was sent to find, borne by those he had freed.

Francisco removed the pouch of dust from his shoulder bag and began a ritual. He bowed to the directions, ending with the West, the direction from which Wu had come and the direction in which souls departed.

"Thank you for my friend who was with me for so long. Thank you for the gift of time and redemption."

Francisco looked toward JR and Maria.

"Thank you for this man and this woman who are here to carry on and thank you for their children who we pray can carry on."

At eye level, ravens glided by on the updrafts from the rock's face.

Francisco finished his ritual. He turned and escorted Maria to one of the stone benches where he helped her to sit. He then moved to the railing and tossed a bit of the dust into the uplifting wind. JR watched as the fine talc-like dust rose in the wind and glistened in the sunlight. Suddenly he felt a rap on his back.

He was soaring in the air over the canyon and looked back at himself standing on top of the rock. JR turned his gaze from side to side and discovered his black wings.

JR circled and watched as Francisco walked over to Maria and gently rapped her on the back with the staff. A smile spread over her face as she gazed out over the vast canyon and he could see the flash of green from her earrings.

JR heard a sound to his left, a croaking raven sound, and turned to see another great black bird flying next to him. He felt Maria's presence and knew he wasn't flying alone. Below them Francisco moved to the railing and tossed the remaining dust into the wind and leaned on his staff.

The two birds noticed another raven fly across their path. It took the lead and guided them through the silvery cloud of dust and light, the essence of both Wu and Dizang. The dust settled on their feathers and the wind carried the remainder of the silver cloud down canyon toward the distant valley.

After soaring back and forth over the river thousands of feet below, Maria returned to her bench. She surveyed the other windborne ravens and the canyon before her, then touched her rounded belly. It was a strange path to get here, touching both earth and sky.

Words appeared in Maria's mind, ones that Francisco had taught her, words that she began to sing in the language of her ancestors. When she began singing, Francisco looked over at her with tears. It was no longer a song of wistful pleas and mourning, but rather one of celebration.

I will be anything
Hah-nah nahn een-ah nah-ne
Hah-nah nahn een-ah nah-ne
Hah-nah nahn een-ah nah-ne
Hah-nah nahn een-ah a-a

I will be anything –
crow, rock, stick,
rattlesnake or anything –
if our ones who are dead
could come back
to us, in this world.

The dance had worked its magic and JR was no longer a ghost. He'd come back from the dead and the world was better, the landscape absolved of his debt.

JR alighted back on the rock and walked toward her.

Elements of Being vi

Time passes, the face wrinkles, folds in the universe appear. Focus the mind and step through the opening. Time is practice for no-time. The immortal's body wrinkles and dies, but the immortal does not. Practice, practice while there is the illusion of time.

Wu Jiyan

RETURN

Wu stood watching the gentle flow of the river before him for a few moments before he noticed the log that spanned the moving water. He leaned on his staff for support as he walked down the riverbank and over to the log. He felt sorrow that Francisco wasn't with him, but knew they'd see each other soon where time didn't matter. Francisco could appear around any corner. Across the river, lush, verdant growth spread along the river and on up a gentle hillside to a mountainous horizon. He could see willows and sycamores along the water, but further up the hillside the trees changed. They looked almost like the trees he knew in China, but he couldn't know for sure until he got there. High above everything jagged peaks protruded through wispy clouds, the mountaintops bathed in golden light and looking like a dragon in repose. From over the mountain behind him he could hear Maria's song.

Wu set foot on the log as he pushed off his staff and began slowly walking across the river. No matter where he was on the log, his staff seemed to touch the riverbed and keep him balanced without effort. He stopped in the middle for a few moments to study the river and to take in the colors and forms of existence and hold them in his mind.

When he reached the other side of the river, Wu parted the willows and made his way toward a stand of sycamores that in turn yielded to oak. As he walked through the trees the world around him began to change. All about him the branches and leaves became arms of glowing nebulae that reached into the blackness of space. Stars hung like jewels in his mind.

Wu knew that with each footstep the world he perceived would change until he reached the undivided, unchanging world. He was free to move about in any direction, from the divided to the undivided, and back again, to the left or to the right. Wu studied the shifting cosmos, knowing he could return to the river and cross to the other side again if needed. His staff would help him remember the way if he decided to go back and dance the crying dance again for the redemption of all beings.

He smiled at the image of JR and Maria in the world, her song in his mind.

The fabric of the Great Mind rippled around him as he passed and made accommodation upstream and downstream to allow for his existence and for the swirling, shifting nuance of the Story, both in and out of time.

BENEDICTION

Without a body or a mind, there is no change, the plotline of the Great Mind unrealized among the stars. Embrace being. This is the Story. Turn it over in your mind, carry it with you. Carry it with you and add to the Story. Toss your words and awareness and art back to the source like a fire casting its light back to the waiting stars and free all those in hell.

Find your praise for existence.

My words are tied in one
with these great mountains,
With the great rocks,
with the great trees,
In one with my body
and my heart.
Do you all help me
with supernatural power,
And you, day,
and you, night!
All of you see me
one with this world!

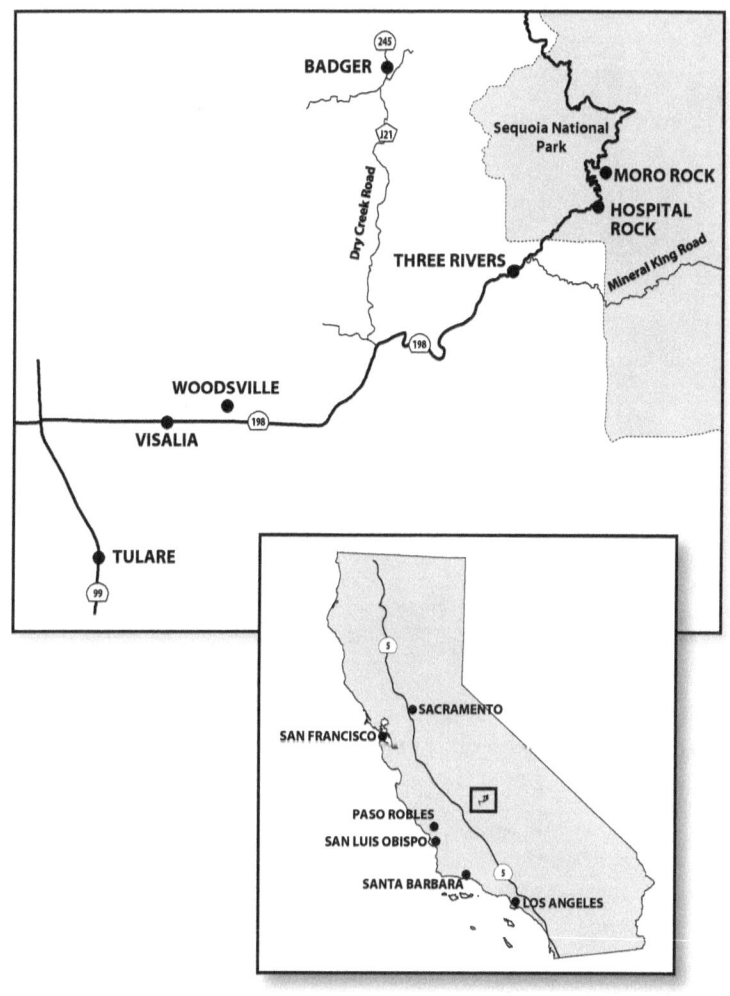

ACKNOWLEDGMENTS

My deep appreciation to Matthew Rangel for accompanying me on my jaunts around Tulare County where I discovered what wanted to be written. Thanks also to his wife Amie for putting up with my visits.

Thanks to Jack Huneke and Julie Harcos of the Stonehouse Residency of the Arts in Miramonte, CA for hosting me as I worked on this book

Gratitude to Mark Schannon for being a friend, and for offering his insight into the manuscript.

Thanks to James King and Alice Alldredge for their multilevel support for this project.

I'm indebted to John Dofflemyer for the use of his poem "Still in the Mountains." I'm always moved by the eloquence of the words.

Finally, thanks to Dr. Charles Raison for exploring with me the past, present, and future of the San Joaquin Valley and of the human mind.